FREE PERIOD

ALI TERESE

Scholastic Press

New York

Library of Congress Cataloging-in-Publication Data available

ISBN 978-1-338-83583-0

10 9 8 7 6 5 4 3 2 1   24 25 26 27 28

Printed in Italy   183
First edition, March 2024
Book design by Maeve Norton

For Teenie

# CHAPTER 1

WINNING

HELEN

Late April, eighth grade, aka two months to FREEDOM

I love gym. Where else can you drive jocks absolutely bonkers without sweating?

The sweat thing was key. I still had math after gym, final bell, and the bus ride home to get through. I meant to do it pristinely. We didn't have it as bad as first-period gym—I assume those kids have wronged our principal severely over multiple past lives to get that kind of schedule—but still. Gross.

It was a week after spring break, but rain poured down outside, so the game du jour was volleyball. Coach Kline must have thought he had finally found a way to get me "involved" when he made me a captain, but I immediately called my team "This Side of the Net Doesn't Sweat." Most of the girls, and even a couple of boys, joined me. I kept checking the door for Gracie, my best friend, but she was nowhere to be seen. Instead, I stared down our archnemesis Madison, the rest of the jocks, and some triers. Not exactly lions versus zebras. More like vultures versus kids counting on high school being much better than this.

After we successfully missed six consecutive balls, Coach Kline forced the other team to rotate. Madison grabbed the ball, pushed up her bangles, and pulled her arm back to serve under-hand. Not what I expected. The ball barely cleared the net and hit the floor. Her next serve went into our second row, hit a new(ish) girl's arm, and flew out of bounds.

"Ouch," Larisa said, grabbing her elbow. Might as well have been the smell of blood for the vultures.

"Yeah! Get it!" yelled the jock horde. Bless those boys. Where do they come from? Maybe there is an elaborate scam where someone slips a note on their lunch trays that says, *An international sportsball scout is coming to gym today. Time to dazzle!*

Madison did get it. Again and again, she served to Larisa, who finally tried putting her arms together to bump the ball back, but she got hurt again. Time for me to do some captaining.

"Madison will keep hitting it at you, so focus on the ball, watch it leave her hand, and as it comes over the net, you slide out of the way," I said. It felt good to contribute.

Everyone else on our side already knew what was up. We were a perfect ballet of avoidance, all of us swaying like reeds in the wind. And there was a bonus. Nothing makes jocks go more feral than not playing their game. A few even growled. It was glorious.

The score reached 15–0. Time to switch sides. Right then, like an angel descending through a cosmic storm, Gracie popped through the gym doors. She waved at me and skipped over to the net. She still hadn't changed out of her street clothes. Strictly verboten.

"Where have you been?" I asked and gave her a bear hug. When middle school started, our schedules had matched completely. This year we only had half our classes together. I hadn't seen her since lunch or five billion years ago. It was hard to tell.

"Nurse. I'm period cramping too bad for gym. She gave me a note and an ice pack," Gracie said.

"Isn't exercise supposed to help?" I whispered.

"That's what Big Gym wants us to believe. They wouldn't be all *get running* if we were bleeding out of anywhere else. I tried to get you a note too, but she said best friends don't get sympathy cramps."

The crimson wave wouldn't hit me again for a while. It was ridiculous our cycles weren't in sync, even if the science is still out on that whole phenomenon. It was also ridiculous that Gracie was more comfortable talking about my period than I was. I'd go for something classic, like a good rash no one's seen since the 1800s, before telling the nurse I was cramping.

There was no time to wallow over my womb, though. Madison was up in my personal space, trying to drape her arm over my shoulder even though I'm half a foot taller than her and practically everyone else at school.

"Will your team actually start playing now, Helen? We have the pep rally and county Cheerfest this Thursday. I want all the cardio I can get," Madison said. Then she leaned close to my bestie and sniffed.

"We're going to high school soon, Gracie. Time for you to explore the antiperspirant aisle."

Gracie raised her arm and took a long, deep breath. "Lavender lemon all-natural rock deodorant. Better than strolling into a spa. Come on, Madison, get in my armpit."

Coach Kline blew his whistle and jogged over to a chorus of jock "yos."

"What's the holdup, ladies?" he said.

"Gracie stinks and clearly needs a health class refresher on personal grooming," Madison said matter-of-factly. It was mortifying that I'd ever been friends with her, even if it was just playdates back in elementary school. Every day of middle school, Madison had another cutting comment, another takedown of someone minding their own business, another reason to avoid her, but attacking Gracie and bringing a teacher into it—a dude, no less? This meant war.

Gracie raised her arm again. "Coach, it is like frolicking through a field of flowers."

"You girls should be more supportive of each other. Social. Emotional. Empower."

I wasn't sure if he was having some sort of brain event or saying every "girl" word he'd ever heard.

"I'm an expert on wellness," Madison said, crossing her arms. "It does not require everyone in class having to smell you."

"My moms don't want me absorbing heavy metals like aluminum," Gracie said. "I mean, we're mammals, we're meant to sweat." She laughed, but she brought her arms down real close to her sides and looked at me with those baby browns that are slightly too big for her face and way too big for my heart.

That's when I knew. If Madison was so bothered by smells, I would serve her one she'd never forget.

"This is a middle school gym, Madison, everything stinks," Coach Kline said. "Go to your side. Sasso, follow her."

Gracie doubled over, clutched the ice pack to her stomach, and handed him the nurse's note. "Ms. Shapiro said I can be the timer."

"There are no time limits in volleyball," Coach Kline said.

"How existential."

"You skipped in here just fine."

"Well, the cramps aren't in my legs."

"Another prank—"

"If this is a prank, blame Mother Nature, not me."

Coach Kline looked at the clock. "Stand somewhere on Helen's side, and we'll call it a wash."

He may have been a grown man wearing striped soccer shorts to his job, but he knew how to pick his battles. I love well-trained adults.

Except there was a twist. As I scooted under the net, Coach Kline tossed me the ball.

"I'm allergic to leather," I said.

"It's synthetic," Coach Kline said. Then he whispered, "I know what you're capable of, and I expect you to play."

He must have seen the disbelief on my vexed visage because he hissed, "Seward Park courts."

I gasped. "That's two towns over."

"It's where I live."

"Teachers are allowed to cross town lines?"

"Serve it, Wells."

This was not part of my no-sweating plan. Here's the thing: Seward Park is where Dad forces me and my little sister to play tennis on Sundays. Family time, if you can even imagine it for a group of people who barely talk to one another. What saves me is that I'm actually good at tennis. All of it. I got ground game, my serve rocks, and I can even put top spin on the ball. Dad mistakes this awesomeness for me making an effort, which makes him ridiculously happy. But it's really just like my DNA got together and said, *Okay, we'll do it if you leave us alone the rest of the week.*

I held the ball in my left hand and drew my right arm down, ready to serve it underhand. Coach Kline coughed loudly and shook his head. Diabolical. That made me want to hit it out of bounds even more, but I had no idea what gym punishment might look like. More gym? OMG!

I threw the ball up and sent it over the net the way I would in tennis. The jocks went wild.

"Get it!"

"Dig it!"

"Set me up!"

They were all so excited the ball fell in the middle of them and hit the floor.

Now, raising your hand over your head to hit one ball may not lead to sweat, but two was risking it, and three would have turned me into a farm animal. Admittedly, my parents didn't care if I absorbed an entire mine's worth of aluminum through my pits, but I can't stand feeling clammy.

I was calculating the angle that I'd have to hit the ball to make it bounce out the gym door and ricochet down the hallway to put an end to this horror when the unthinkable happened. Larisa, that girl Madison kept hitting, started clapping.

"Go Helen!" she said.

What was Larisa thinking? I looked over to Gracie.

"Um, yeah! Ball Things, Helen! Team Sayings!" she added to Larisa's cheers.

It was WEIRD. Still, I got some butterflies in my stomach, a thump-thump in my heart. I threw the ball higher this time and hit it into the back row, right next to Madison. She put her hands together and tried to dig it, but the ball bounced off her and into the back wall. She re-tucked her shirt to a bunch of "Come ons!" from the jocks and polite clapping from our side.

A dilemma. Being my mortal enemy is one thing. Getting yelled at by those turds was another. If you're sending a ball hurtling through the air at approximately 40 mph, how do you decide between aiming at a mean girl or a bunch of jerk boys? All I could think was, everyone should get theirs in their natural habitat. Madison could wait.

This time, I threw the ball real high and stepped into the serve. The ball exploded off my palm and spiked the dude next to Madison so fast he never had a chance to move. For the boy next to him I landed it right at his feet. I was still working my way through the front row when the whistle blew. I held the ball on my hip and tried to catch my breath. The last few minutes of class had elapsed at warp speed. My teammates patted me on the back and threw in a few "good jobs" as we headed toward the locker room. I was all "whatever," of course, but one of those butterflies kept fluttering in my belly.

Gracie put her arm around my shoulders. "You were awesome out there. And you really worked up a sweat."

"Don't rub it in," I said and hugged Gracie back, but kept my eyes on Madison.

CHAPTER 2

DONUTS MAKE
THE DREAM WORK

GRACIE

After school, Donut Hour

Helen and I had set aside that entire afternoon to plan the most epic prank ever to close out our Darlington Middle School careers. As we sat with our shared maple log and matching iced hot chocolates at the Cruller Castle, the premier donut destination in our little town, I couldn't help but get a little emotional. To think that it all started when our friendship burst to life on the first day of fifth grade. Helen getting yelled at by the lunch monitor for launching spitballs at me with her straw in the caf. Me sliding my tray down to her end of the table and showing her how there's no evidence left behind if you use tiny pieces of chewed-up ice that melt when they land instead of paper bits. We joined forces to face the world, launch ice-chip spitballs at the lunch monitor, and be friends forever.

I spit a shard of ice from my drink at Helen across the donut-shaped table.

"Ouch," she said, rubbing her neck. "Nice shot, though."

"Only for you, bestie," I said and pulled out my supplies.

Brainstorming is too violent a concept for my taste. I prefer

8

"synapse swirling" and "glitter braining," where all the confetti between my gray-matter cells jiggles together and amazing ideas burst out. When I work, I cut out pictures from ancient fashion mags, use every color gel pen and eye shadow in the rainbow, and make my own props. For today's noggin-noodling session, I'd made a gorgeous deck of high-jinks cards to get the creative juices gushing. Now I laid them out before us. Fun was the main goal, but for our final prank, it wouldn't be awful to do something big enough to be remembered for.

"Yellow cards are for the Place, pink are for the Action—" I began.

"And orange for the Target," Helen said.

"I think of them more as the prank's Beneficiary. Pick one of each color and you have a plan. Remember, the cards are just inspo. This is our middle school prank graduation—"

"Prankuation?" Helen said, diving into our donut.

"Perfection. My point is, anything goes." I pulled three cards to illustrate. "Booger plus Lunch plus Teacher. Insta-prank."

"I love it, but too close to when your snot rocket hit Ms. Varone in the face while she was sipping that tank-size tea at field day," Helen said. She pulled three cards. "Toilet plus Banana Peel plus Mean Girls. Actually, I sort of just set that up in the bathroom here."

And then we were interrupted.

"Hello classmates," chirped Isabella from our English class. "I was heading to the Turret to sit with everyone. Want to come?"

"Prefer it here in the Dungeon with the other peasants," Helen said.

"Me too, actually," Isabella whispered, sliding next to me on the bench seat and nearly hitting my head with her twirling baton. "Are you okay, Gracie?"

Dodging flying objects was actually a nice little adrenaline rush. But the truth was that I did not feel fantastic. My cramps had been getting worse as the day went on. Under normal circumstances I would have asked Helen to come over to my house and throw cheeseballs into my mouth like I was a seal while I pressed my bloated belly into a pillow on the floor. But the parentals were being so absurd lately with their maybe-you-need-to-expand-your-social-circle hints and the stop-always-getting-in-trouble-with-Helen direct blows. Like our hearts have any say in whether the friends we'd follow to the end of the universe are into rules or not.

"It's just the patriarchy in my gut, but thanks for asking. Why are you all wet?" I asked. Isabella's neon pink tracksuit was dripping from our bench seat onto the floor.

"There was soap squirted in front of the stalls for some reason," she explained, pointing her baton back at the shop's bathroom doors. "Maybe I should try to dry myself a bit more. Watch my donut and twirl my baton?"

I gave her a nod and Helen a look.

"She is not a Mean Girl," I said.

Helen grabbed Isabella's donut and started eating the jelly out with a spoon. "She's within the Cheersphere."

"It isn't about Cheer," I said. "It is about being a Madison follower. The girls under her spell would be just as cringe if they were all in an evil chess club."

Helen's eyebrows arched. "Now I want to start an evil chess club, except I don't want to learn chess or be part of anything."

"Of course not, ew. But Isabella is always nice to us, and I like her pattern instincts. She really knows how to clash," I said, tossing the baton back and forth between my hands.

"And soap isn't a 'Banana Peel,'" Helen said, holding up that prank card, "which is why I said I 'sort of' did that. Back to planning. How about Drop-Off plus Fart plus Parents?"

It all felt like small potatoes. Don't get me wrong. I love hotboxing my moms on a Sunday morning, but this was supposed to be a prank worthy of our legacy, not squeezing out a Silent Sammy before sliding out of the back seat at the school entrance. I pawed through the cards for something exciting to grab me by the nostrils and not let go until I was grounded for a week.

Isabella plopped back in her seat, slightly less damp, and took back her baton as I pulled the Locker, Chaos, and Smarties cards.

"How would you feel," Helen asked Isabella, "about finding your locker lock in a box mixed in with everyone else's locks and you had to check them all to find yours?"

I got all choked up. Switching locks on people was my absolute favorite pastime, and here was Helen taking it to the next level.

Isabella's baton spun faster. "Are you doing that to me?"

"Never you specifically," I said. "More of the general 'you.'"

She relaxed. "Actually, if it was everyone's locks, the office has a list of the serial numbers and would just match the locks to the names. So, I would be bummed and confused, but not too bothered. Wait, why is there no jelly in my jelly donut?" Isabella held it up to the light.

"This place isn't what it used to be," Helen said.

Isabella leaned across the table, took a perfectly manicured finger, and used it to pluck a glob of jelly off Helen's cheek. The distance between us all grew dry and electric. I had to act.

"Have no fear!" I blurted out. "I brought enough petite madeleines from home to share."

I got the pastry box from my bag. Baking is my happy place, and lately I needed to hang out there more and more.

"They're the most beautiful little things I've ever seen," Isabella gushed as she picked up a madeleine. "Are they wearing highlighter?"

"I wanted them to match my look," I said, framing my cheeks in my hands.

"You're blinding. I haven't been able to look directly at you all day," Helen said.

"My goal was for me and the cookies to be so luminous, people on the International Space Station would be like, *Whoa, it's a little bright down there*." I leaned over and pointed at the cookie Isabella was still admiring. "See? Inverted mini-choco chips for the eyes and nose, the eensiest strawberry slice for the pouty mouth, and a mirror glaze for the cheeks. Do you want another?"

"Ugh," Isabella said, her gaze shifting from her cookie to her phone. "I have to go. Madison just called another Cheer practice on her lawn."

"Tell her no. She's not in charge of you," Helen said.

"Technically, no. Practically, she's in charge of everyone,"

Isabella said and grabbed her bag. "Gracie, love the cookies. Helen, love the grrrrrr."

And then there were two. It was time to get serious.

"What about waiting for the graduation ceremony?" I suggested. "I don't like giving the fifth through seventh graders a free pass, but we'd prank a considerable number of parents."

"Love the crowd idea . . ." Helen sat up straighter on her side of the booth. "What about the pep rally on Thursday?"

"I just assumed we'd be cutting then. Besides, this is an end-of-the-year prank. We're still in April."

Helen flipped all the cards over and swished them around on the table. She pulled: Gym, Skunk, and Everyone.

"Stink," Helen said.

"Stank," I said.

"Skunk," Helen said. "Before we cut, we set things up so at just the right time, a smell takes over the gym. One so foul, everyone will think about it for years."

"Like they go to take a whiff of their newborn's head in twenty years and all they get is this stink," I said. Really, it was quite sad to think of all the people who didn't get to be best friends with an actual genius. "Okay, doing an April prank is growing on me. Go big now and then just coast until June? A few pencils greased here, a teacher planner superglued to the table there, but otherwise the pressure is off."

"We deserve a rest," Helen said.

I leaned back and chewed my ice chips. "Two problems. First, three days is not a lot of time to get a skunk who'd want to get involved."

"Not a real skunk. No one can get a skunk," Helen said.

"Sure you can. Being allowed to own a pet skunk is one of the main reasons my Uncle Gerald lives in this state. But I would never put his Heloise in that kind of position. It will have to be artificial but nontoxic."

"Perfect," Helen said. "You're in charge of the stink. I'll cover the delivery mechanism. What was the second problem?"

"Why didn't we do this last week? It would have been Stink Break instead of Spring Break!"

CHAPTER 3

STANK

HELEN

Thursday, seventh period, aka one hour to an early prankuation

I didn't even complain when Coach Kline made me a field hockey captain for gym. I was too busy looking forward to Gracie and me slipping back into the school to set up our prank for the last-period pep rally, giving Madison and her Cheer squad the world's stinkiest send-off for their county competition. I used my time as captain wisely, hip-checking every jock at least once. Finally, the whistle blew.

"She got me in the stomach, Coach!" Jasper cried from the grass.

I gave the whiny baby a hand up. "The perks of being a tall girl."

"Pleasantly shocked by the enthusiasm, Wells, but you can't check someone who doesn't have the ball," Coach said. "Also, you can't check anyone, because we're in gym."

"It's fine, I have to take a dump anyway," I said and handed him my stick.

Gracie sat up from where she'd been sunbathing in midfield. "Me too."

Coach launched into a soliloquy on class disruption, our responsibility to use the toilet in the thirty-four seconds we have

15

between classes, and the need for team cohesion. Imagine the brainpower to be saved if these adults trusted us to use the bathroom when we needed to. Not that I actually needed to use the bathroom, but still.

Gracie gently interrupted him. "It was Sloppy Joe Day."

Coach reconsidered things mid-sentence. The look on his face told me he too had experienced the eternal question of whether sweet cafeteria meat of unknown origin was worth the inevitable intestinal distress and made the same bad decision I always did.

"All right," he relented, "but get back here quick to circle up. Somewhere between sleeping on the field and sucker-punching your classmates, I think one of you will score."

I locked my arm in Gracie's and turned us toward the building.

"Why is it always circle up to score and never for anything good, like summoning a spirit?" she said.

"Will summoning a stink do?" I said.

I'd been up most of the night putting the finishing touches on my carefully calibrated contribution to the prank: a stink-diffusion apparatus with chambers on each end to hold the stinks before they mixed in the middle, where a tiny fan would release them into the world. The compression sleeve was outfitted with a timer so we could set it up and be long gone before deployment. Laying everything out on the locker room bench, I felt this weird twinge of pride.

"Gracie?" I whispered.

She slammed a locker door closed, revealing that she'd changed into a glittery black velour jumpsuit, her long black hair spilling out from the cinched hood. When she turned to take an over-the-shoulder selfie, I noticed the back of the jumpsuit was covered in blinding rhinestone letters spelling LA PUZZA.

"Nice, right? Means 'The Stink,'" she said.

"It isn't exactly incognito. We never discussed outfits."

"Well, you look ridiculously gorgeous always. I'm just trying to keep up," she said, blowing me air kisses. Everyone deserves a best friend who makes you feel like a movie star when you're sporting stained khakis and last year's field day T-shirt.

"Plus, I couldn't leave the house in it this morning," she went on. "Moms were doing sunrise yoga and thought I'd dressed to join them." Gracie got out an eyeliner pencil and began drawing whiskers from her nose across her cheeks. "It's like they're trying to make sure my gag reflex still works, in case they ever need to leave me alone around small objects."

"Shhhhh." I could have sworn I'd heard something, even though we should have had the locker room to ourselves for another half hour.

Gracie dropped her voice to a whisper that was still somehow louder than most people talk. "Did your parentals ask what this equipment was all about?"

I gave her the universal sign for *zip it* and wondered why we bothered spending all of winter break working on our telepathy if she refused to use it. There was nothing to tell, anyway. My parents and little sister barely looked up from their cereal bowls when I'd jetted out that morning. If I'm not causing trouble, I might as well be invisible.

And that's when I saw it. A flash of neon coming down the aisle.

"Duck," I said.

Gracie stuck her lips out and pouted over her shoulder for another selfie.

"No, not duck face," I said, pulling her down behind the bench with me. Maybe it was the head custodian, Mr. Allen. Maybe it was a kid who had a real sloppy-joe stomachache. I only hoped it wasn't Madison—who'd been missing at gym—or one of the other cheerleaders.

Just then, a shadow cast over us. I looked up to find Ruth and Mary Miller, the most popular girls in school. If Darlington Middle were the savanna, these girls were lionesses and Gracie and I were rabid honey badgers they liked to share a lunch carcass with occasionally.

"Hey idiots," they said in unison.

"You two are looking very fluorescent," Gracie said as we stood back up. "A whole administrative vibe with the safety vests that I'm loving."

"With great office assistant power comes a great big smock. What are you doing in here?" Ruth said.

"More importantly," Mary chimed in, "you're coming over this weekend, right? It's quiz night, and you missed the last one."

These girls could have hung out with anyone they wanted. They were rich and had nice clothes and an entire pool in their backyard. For some reason they picked us as sleepover pals last year. I didn't question it too much because hanging with the Miller twins was actually fun—they had awesome snacks and their parents never actually made us go to sleep even when I would have preferred to—but they were also a lot. There was no way I could handle one of their weird homemade quizzes and noogiefests after not sleeping last night to build our device.

"Sorry, Ruth—" I started.

"The quiz we made is deep," Ruth said, ignoring me. "Question 1: You're on a desert island, there's one piece of cheesecake, but to get it you either have to listen to your grandpa's heavy metal albums for an hour or drink a glass of salt water. What do you do?"

"Be thankful I am against soft cheeses in the first place," I said.

Gracie looked dead serious. "You are well aware of my long-term relationship with soft cheeses, but I love salt water. Give it to me. I don't even need the cake. But I have an exclusive fashion-baking-not-quizzing thing Friday."

Mary rolled her eyes. "You're so hilarious. I took your phone during math and your calendar was empty Friday. Shocker. And Helen, you're like a fourth grader with no phone. If Gracie isn't busy, you don't have anything to do."

Just then the twins' walkie-talkies went off in unison. Principal Varone's voice droned out, "Another batch of deliveries to make, girls."

Mary took the stack of papers in her hand and tossed them in the garbage while Ruth chirped over the speaker, "We just finished the first. On our way!"

"Are you going to tell we were in here?" I said.

"Just leave us out of whatever weird thing you freaks are doing," Mary said.

•   •   •

Gracie and I slipped into the gym with my apparatus and her stink blubs, which she refused to call "bombs" because she said that word was too harsh. The room felt cavernous. No one grunting. No one twirling their hair, willing the clock to turn faster. Most importantly, no bleachers. I expected—needed—the bleachers to be extended in preparation for the pep rally, but they were still pushed flat against the wall.

"Helen!" Gracie had found some huge rolls of paper stacked on vertical stands next to boxes of art supplies. "The universe is asking us to craft. Let's make dresses like we're paper dolls." She started pulling out the end of an orange roll taller than her.

Before I could remind her about our mission, the doors at the far end of the gym burst open. Three girls dressed in cheerleading skirts and sporting headache-inducing ponytails marched in. There was nowhere to hide. Then I heard Gracie's voice from behind the orange paper.

"Just roll with it," she whispered, waving to me from inside the orange paper roll. I immediately pulled on the blue paper and rolled myself inside. I clenched my eyes shut as the squeak of sneakers stopped next to us.

"Today will be the best Cheerfest ever. I demand the best pep rally with the best signs ever to celebrate us."

Madison. Of course.

"But I can't choose. What color would you pick?" said another voice.

"School colors, Ashley. Obviously," said Avery, another of Madison's followers.

My heart dropped. Those were the colors—Sunrise Orange and Atlantic Blue—Gracie and I had wrapped ourselves in. There were seconds to decide between busting out monster-style or letting them find me.

"Hold up, Avery," Madison said. "School colors are obvious, which is why we won't use them."

"Wow. You're so right, Madison. Like all the time," Ashley said.

"Let's go with yellow. Bright, full of hope, and as close as you can get to gold, which is what we'll be bringing home. These losers could use something exciting."

"We're such a treasure," Ashley said.

"We give them H-O-P-E," Avery said.

More meanness for no reason. I wanted to run through the paper, tackle Madison to the floor, and fart in her face until she knew what a stink really meant. But I'd made a plan, so I willed myself to be patient as I listened to them tear the paper and finally skip away, out of the gym.

I unfurled myself at last, then tugged the orange roll to spin out my best friend.

"Are you okay?" I asked.

Gracie checked herself. "Phew, no paper cuts."

"No, I mean about Madison. She is a demon. And demons are meant to stink. Let's make that happen for her," I said.

"But not her specifically," Gracie said.

"Why not? Madison made fun of you over deodorant, and Coach did nothing. I'm sick of her getting away with everything."

"I haven't even thought about that since then, why are you?

21

Uh-oh, I thought we were just having fun. This is our PhD prank, Helen. Not revenge," Gracie said.

"It is pranking with purpose," I said and turned before she could argue with me.

Opening the bleachers was now the riskiest part of the operation. I used my key chain lockpick to open the button's compartment. The bleachers whirred, expanding from the wall, but not too loudly. There was time to get in, install the stink blubs, and shut them again before anyone else came in.

"Just stick it anywhere," Gracie said as we scurried underneath the seats.

I kept going until I counted to the bench where Madison would perch.

Gracie handed me two little bottles.

"I split the stink into two parts, as your amazing brain suggested. For one, I stuck a pin into an egg, which then baked in the sun," she said, raising one full of green, yellow, and brown ooze before handing me another that was suspiciously clear. "The other is artificial skunk essence. No Heloises were harmed in the commission of this prank."

"How revolting. I love you." I attached a blub to each end of the diffuser and slid the compression sleeve over everything. The final step was connecting the timer before we duct-taped it all to the bleachers.

"Hold the setup so I can use my teeth on the duct tape," I said to Gracie. There were only a few more minutes before everyone would come in from gym to change.

"Ooohhhh," she said. "It is super squishy!"

Gracie had one hand on each side of the compression sleeve, squeezing away. Of course it was squishy. I'd stayed up all night designing and building the sleeve so when the timer went off, the sleeve would compress, sending the liquids from each side into the center chamber to mix, and then mist out through the diffuser.

The two liquids entered the chamber. The little fan in the diffuser pushed the scent out.

"Oh," Gracie said.

Just then the bleacher machinery started whirring. The benches came toward us fast. I grabbed Gracie's hand and we ran toward the wall. But by the time we got there, we were trapped. Gracie was still holding our stink blub. I grabbed it from her hand and jammed it between the bleacher and the wall. There was just enough space to spare for our bodies as the stink of skunks and rotten eggs washed over us.

CHAPTER 4

BODACIOUS BAKING
& DELICIOUS DECORATING

GRACIE

Thursday night après stink, Sugar Hour

I highly recommend the First Rule of Drool mobile pet grooming service if you ever find yourself smelling like a lactose-intolerant rodent that fell into an industrial tub of Rocky Road and had to eat her way out.

After the school sent me and Helen home, I was not allowed inside. Mama made me stay on the lawn like I was a naughty labradoodle (I wish!), so I laid down in the grass to air out and watch the clouds float by, which I swear were all shaped like skunks.

When the groomer screeched her van to a stop in the drive-way, my moms came back out. There was yelling and crying, a call to poison control over the de-skunk shampoo ingredient list, and, finally, a massive basin. The groomer filled it with a million bubbles that I jumped right into. It was uber relaxing. I should bathe on the lawn more often.

But even after I was fully de-skunked, they were still upset. What was so interesting is they were yelling at each other *about me* more than they yelled *at me*. Like Mama didn't even cross-examine me like she usually does. Eventually she did reach I'm-going-for-a-drive mad, which is like her Level 11, basically the maddest I ever see her. Mommy followed her to the driveway. I was deep into my go-to de-stressors—a makeover and matching bakeover—when Mommy came back inside. My body tensed up before she said anything. And stayed tense, even after she hugged me. The worst.

"What are we calling this look?" she asked, wiping some of my green makeup from her own cheek.

"Zombie baker making zombie skunk cupcakes. I've got a green matte base for my whole face, the dirt splotches are cocoa powder, and I'm hoping I can get the leftover gummy worms to stick to my cheeks like they're crawling out of my skin."

"Deliciously disturbing," Mommy said.

She picked up the fondant diagrams I'd drawn to change the strawberry shortcake cupcakes we made earlier in the week into something more in line with my current aura.

"We should talk about what happens next," Mommy said as I pulled more ingredients from my Sugar Cabinet.

"I know, right? You're asking yourself when do we bake the gummy worms inside the cupcake? Never! We hollow out the already baked cupcakes and put the worms and jam in the middle."

Mommy put her hand on mine. She squeezed it.

Ugh.

Talk incoming.

"I meant what comes next in your life, Gracie. Today was a major wake-up call. You're growing up."

I started making zombie groans, but she put her hand over my mouth.

"You're pulling away from us. I barely know what's going on in that head of yours anymore."

"That makes two of us."

"It is all developmentally appropriate," Mommy said, using her softest pediatrician voice on me. "We want to support you and respect your freedom, but I'm concerned that you're using that freedom to choose Helen. In a way, you're replacing us with Helen."

"Mommy, jealousy is an ugly look, even on a gorgeous gal like you," I said.

Besides, it isn't freedom if you just do what your moms want you to do. That's called turning into your parentals. Shudder.

"I know you didn't have this kind of soulmate bestie—" I continued.

"I have a sister—"

"Who you don't talk to."

It almost looked like she flinched when I said it. The worst worstens.

"Oh, I'm sorry, Mommy, that was harsh."

"That's all right. My point is that you need to be your own person. Not following us, not following your friend, but following your own journey," Mommy said.

"That's a little too schmaltzy even for me, and I am a girl in this world molding marzipan into tiny demonic skunk zombies."

"Think about what I said and what you'll tell the principal tomorrow."

She hugged me again. It was different this time. Like she was searching for something she could only find with our hearts pressed together.

I didn't hug her back.

A couple hours later I snuck out my bedroom window and was cutting through the usual lawns on my way to Helen's house, armed with nothing but a pastry box and hope, when I walked right into a boy from my health class.

"Fancy meeting you here, Michael F.," I said.

"You know, Gracie, most people just call me Mike," he said. "Like, everyone other than you. And this is my backyard."

"You live right next to my best friend, Helen Wells," I said, in awe of how really tiny this universe is.

He took off his glasses and cleaned them using the tail of his button-down utility shirt. "For a few years. Usually, I see you cutting through from my window. Really liked that day when you made your eyes look like butterfly wings, but this undead thing is cool, too," he said.

"You know that comment is getting you a zombie-skunk cupcake," I said, opening the pastry box.

Michael F. took the skunk off and put it in his pocket.

"That little guy is marzipan. He's edible," I said.

"Yeah, but . . . I want to save it," Michael F. said.

Then he took a massive bite of cupcake. The look of total and complete shock told me he'd made it to the worms and jam.

"Sweet and vile," he said, still chewing. "I want to vomit, but I also want to keep eating."

No one had ever so perfectly gotten my culinary aesthetic before. What was going on with this boy? There was a tent, the cutest mini-grill, and a bunch of other outdoor things I hoped to never know the names of.

I pointed at the tent. "Dude, what did you do? I mean, I've taken up bathing in the yard, which I highly recommend, but even I haven't done anything to make my parents move me outside completely."

He ran his fingers through his hair. "I'm making up for some scouting badges. There isn't enough time between homework and all the clubs and sports to earn them on real camping trips. But I'm so close to finishing this level, and I haven't told my parents I don't want to go for Condor, the next scouting award, yet."

I didn't understand any of the words coming out of his mouth except maybe the prepositions. But it suddenly hit me that Michael F. was a cutie. Not in a he-knows-how-to-dress-himself way, but he had the tousled super-dark brown hair and chunky glasses vibe I never noticed indoors. If I ended up liking outside because of a boy, I would seriously never forgive either of us. But also, he was struggling.

"My family has a saying, *Meglio essere un uccello nel bosco che un uccello nella gabbia d'oro.* It's like, *Better to be a free bird than one in a swank cage.* I think birds are disgusting and wouldn't want to be any kind, but maybe that can help with your whole condor situation," I said.

"Wild and free. I like it. Hey, are you really the reason the pep rally got canceled?" he said.

"Sort of . . . actually, completely. Are you mad, too?"

"Well, it meant we had to stay in history, but the teacher just gave us a silent reading hour."

"I'm not sure if I should be doing a victory dance or groveling for forgiveness. No one's reactions to things are making sense to me today."

He leaned in and whispered, "Silent reading is pretty much my favorite kind of hour, so victory dance."

I felt a little shiver go up my spine. This boy needed to be studied for science, but I had places to be. "I will see you in health tomorrow, Michael F., but now I must find out how the most wonderful creature to ever walk this cursed earth is doing. Ciao ciao!"

I crept over to Helen's first-floor bedroom window and sat under it, waiting for her as dusk settled on the neighborhood. Her lights were out, and I could hear yelling somewhere inside the house. I decided to pre-cupcake with an extra one I'd brought and was about to take a bite when there was a tiny tap on my shoulder.

"She's not in there, and you're not supposed to be out here," Seraphine, Helen's third-grader sister, said in her tiny horror-movie voice. It was always jarring to see her—same chestnut hair as Helen, same cat-about-to-pounce movements, same sprinkling of freckles, but it was all through a miniature, evil filter. That night it didn't help that she loomed over me with one fist of fury dug into her hip, the other shining a flashlight right into my eyes.

"Oh, um, hi, cutie. Want a cupcake?"

She snatched it with her little paw and dug right in, coming up from the bite with red gummies oozing down her chin.

"It is going to take more than sugar to bribe me not to tell Mom and Dad," Seraphine said.

Just then, there was a bunch more shouting, a door slammed, and Helen's window flung open without the lights ever turning on. She stuck her head into the night.

"Out," she hissed at Seraphine.

"I already am out. And I bet Mom and Dad would looooooooove to know Gracie is here."

"What do you want?" Helen asked.

"Justice," Seraphine said.

"I know you'll ransack my room as soon as I leave because you'll know I can't say anything because I was supposed to be in here the whole time."

Seraphine's eyes opened wider and wider until she almost lost her scowl, but then she just scowled harder. "Mr. Wigglesworth," she finally said.

Helen gasped. Helen never gasps.

"You are diabolical," she hissed, disappearing back into her room. She reemerged with a glowworm stuffie and thrust it at her little sister. "Be nice to him."

"I heard them talking about Sage Academy for real," Seraphine said as Helen crawled out her window and onto the lawn.

That got everyone quiet. Sage Academy was an all-girls day and boarding high school a few towns over. I didn't know anyone who'd actually been sent there, but the rumors were that it cost college-levels of money, and only certain kinds of girls went there. Like, ones smart enough to design a car, but also just as likely to steal it for a joyride.

I looked to Helen, expecting her to laugh, but she was staring down Seraphine with a face of steel.

"You're lying, Tiny Terror."

"Mom said it when I had my headphones on. The trick is on all of you because sometimes I just put those things on with no show or music when I want to hear what is really going on," Seraphine said.

"Do you want them to send me away?" Helen asked.

"Not always ... but today I do," Seraphine said. Then she climbed through Helen's window and shut it behind her.

I handed Helen a cupcake. It should be a maximum criminal offense for fondant to look so good and taste so bad. But once I got through it, the cake was perfectly moist and spongy, the butter-cream holding it together was not at all cloying, and the center was really sweet and disgusting.

"Thanks," Helen said. She peeled off her fondant quietly. "Even if Seraphine is telling the truth, it isn't like this is the first time they've threatened to 'send me somewhere.'"

"They would never. One of them would have to take you there every day. Parental driving physics alone says it won't happen. They're just having a mad and don't know how to express them-selves," I said.

"Right? And Mom is still way more worried about money than she is about me. By the way, you continue to be the world's most genius baker. These are sick and *sick*. It feels like I'm eating brains," Helen said.

"It is like you can see directly into my baking soul," I said.

Then we both got real quiet for a while before Helen said, "I'm sorry today went sideways. I should never have planned any-thing out of revenge. I know that kills your heart joy."

"The same thing would have happened if we were stinking things up for fun, which is of course what I thought we were doing." I folded my empty cupcake wrapper into a little hat for Helen. "It is weird, though, me and you not being in sync."

"I don't know if it's that bad," Helen said.

Well, that only made me more uncomfortable, so I changed the subject. "You know my Aunt Carmella."

"The witch," Helen said.

"No, she's just an herbalist who sometimes argues with dead people. Anyway, she used to tell me revenge never works and it is awful for the complexion. Like, even if it hurts the other person, you'll end up in more pain. And scaly."

"Turn the other cheek, then?" Helen said.

"More like, live your best life instead of worrying about theirs. How to do that? I have no idea, but she's the only adult who doesn't talk to me like I'm wearing a diaper, so there you go."

"What do you think will happen tomorrow?" Helen asked.

"Why does everyone keep acting like this is some special line we've crossed?" I said.

It was one stink blub. And one canceled pep rally. And one furi-ous custodian. And one team of super-furious cheerleaders. And one police car. Okay, maybe three police cars, but only one fire truck, and some stinky bleachers we spent an hour scrubbing.

Helen put her hand on mine and squeezed. Ugh.

"Maybe let me do the talking when we get called to the office tomorrow," she said.

CHAPTER 5

TROUBLE

HELEN

Friday before homeroom, aka before too early

Principal Varone's dumpster fire of an office always reeked of lavender. Some people might say that stinky skunks can't be choosers, but I don't care. This was not the French fields of purple flowers lavender. More like someone covering up their lethal farts.

We usually had our little chitchats at her round "talking table" with a box of tissues and a bowl of butterscotch candies. After the stink blubs, though, Gracie and I found ourselves disappearing into massive faux-leather armchairs staring at Ms. Varone across her desk. There were papers, files, old take-out containers, and stress squeezies strewn between us. For someone who so clearly thrived in chaos, you'd think she would be more chill with me and Gracie. You'd be wrong.

I felt my legs melting into the pleather, my arms reaching out to straighten the nameplate on her desk.

"Leave it," Ms. Varone said.

"It's uneven," I said.

"I want it that way. Ladies, for anyone else I'd say that smelling like a skunk would have taught you a lesson. However, I know that you two are immune to such things."

It was nice to work with people who really, really know you.

She sprayed more air freshener and turned her desk fan toward us. "We are lucky neither you nor the bleachers were permanently damaged. Tell me what this latest disaster was all about."

Not how I expected things to start. Ms. Varone wasn't usually interested in motives—it was outcomes that mattered. I struggled with whether to tell her about Madison going after Gracie for the whole deodorant thing. Would she have any interest in finally shutting down the mean girls?

Before I could decide, Gracie said, "Just a little light anarchy to get the blood flowing. Thursdays, amiright?"

Ms. Varone sprayed us again.

I coughed. "My mom scrubbed a few layers of my skin off while her burning rage tears rained down on me. And Gracie got the pampered poodle treatment. We're all good to return to class. Unless you want to call it a year?"

"Don't I wish, but not an option. This kind of vandalism isn't what I expect from you two."

She picked up a folder from her desk. It was about three inches thick.

"Grace Sasso. Tardiness, Insubordination, Insubordination, Tardiness, Code 226—I actually have to look that one up."

"Maybe the day I got to school on time, but remembered how boring it is and left?" Gracie guessed.

Ms. Varone sighed, then opened a slightly smaller file. "Helen Wells. Insubordination, Insubordination, Insubordination, Insubordination . . ."

"I'm never late," I said.

Ms. Varone squared herself to us, crossed her arms over her chest, and rested her elbows on the desk. Disappointed lecture pose. An absolute classic.

"A canceled pep rally," she began. "Athletes are demanding justice. More importantly, their parents are sending me novell-length emails that I am not interested in reading. Time to get serious, girls. The latest research shows that suspensions don't work, and obviously you'd see it as a vacation, anyway. We won't go there yet."

She was clearly a mind reader.

"This incident will go in each of your permanent files."

Didn't sound great.

"Another week of lunch detention."

A given.

"No normal punishment works with you two because you don't care about anything," Ms. Varone said. "Therefore, I am sentencing you to care."

Sentencing me—I mean us—to an emotion? Impossible. I'd only known about it for seconds and my skin was already crawling.

"What about two weeks of lunch detention?" I countered.

"You've spent more time in detention than out over the last four years. It doesn't work. According to the school district's attorney, we are legally obligated to educate you through eighth grade. At that point, a forklift will back up here," she said, gesturing to the window, "to hoist your files to the high school, and I will never need to think about you again."

That was not what I expected to hear. I'd done my research. Our records would be wiped clean after middle school. I was pretty much counting on it. The plan was to hang out and have fun for the next month or so, then figure out how to do whatever we felt like in high school. This whole thing needed to slow down until I could sort through all the puzzle pieces.

But Varone continued, "The question is, how do we get through the rest of the year? I want you to pick something to keep you occupied. Something measurable. You've caused such trouble by not caring, maybe this approach will even be restorative. Perhaps innovative enough to get me in *School Administrator Monthly.* In any event, you have one month to accomplish something that matters to the school."

Gracie squealed and squeezed my hand. "Sounds like a makeover show for our souls! What are we doing?"

How was she going along with this before I had a chance to talk our way out of it? There had to be something in the student handbook, school district policies, state laws, or elemental principles of the universe that would stop us from having to become joiners.

"You pick," Ms. Varone said. "The play? Help with rehearsals and the performance. A sport? Show up for practices and go to the games. A club? It depends on which one—"

Gracie jumped in. "Helen and I can totally join Cupcake Club. I love baking and making animal decorations. I made you one for your birthday, Principal Varone."

"The viper cupcake was from you? Good to know, Gracie. But there is no cupcake club at Darlington Middle School."

It was clear I'd have to drive this thing. "Fine, we'll do Makeup

Club. To be extra do-gooders, maybe we could teach babies how to do makeup."

"Helen made it look like unicorns were being born out of my eyelid creases on our last makeover day. Those babies are so lucky," Gracie said.

Ms. Varone spread her hands on the desk. "Are you telling me that after four years in this school you don't know *any* of our clubs or activities?"

"I want to say there is a Cheesiad, but that may be my brain mushing together something I heard in social studies with the epic cheese competition Helen and I are planning for the summer," Gracie said.

Ms. Varone took a deep breath. "There is Debate Club, Green Team, Mathletes—"

"That would be good for Helen," Gracie cut in, "but it combines my greatest fears—math and doing anything—into a blender and pours them all over my heart joy."

"Chess Club, Golf Clinic, Future Vets—"

"Gracie, I could totally see you in the army someday, let's do that one," I said.

"Vets as in doctors for animals," Ms. Varone said evenly. "Robotics, Magic Club. And, of course, there's Community Action Club, but I hesitate—"

"What does that last one do? I like the action part," I said.

Ms. Varone narrowed her eyes. "They investigate a problem, develop a solution, and bring the school community together to make it happen."

"Like really boring superheroes," Gracie said.

Oh yes, that did sound dull, but with room for some very amorphous accomplishments. I could definitely bluff our way through something that vague.

"We're in," I said.

Ms. Varone tipped back in her chair. She was considering something meaningful to us, that might change our minds, or even the very course of our lives. I knew we had to get this right just in case there was any truth to my parents' delusions about private school. I would happily sit in lunch detention until I needed dentures, but there was no way I could survive being separated from Gracie for all of high school.

The principal shook off whatever it was that gave her pause. She sifted through her desk until she'd scrounged some paper. Then she scribbled something out, stuffed the page in an envelope, and handed it to me.

"Give that to the club leader. Activities Room, today after school. Remember, this is a last chance before I am forced to take more drastic measures. Don't screw it up. Also, get out. It's like sitting across from actual skunks."

I talked my way out of last period that afternoon. It felt like I could finally breathe once the door closed behind me. I love the freedom of the hallway during class. Quiet, empty, reeking of disinfectant, full of possibility. Lessons and gossip alike sealed off in the classrooms. Last period, especially, you can feel the anticipation of final bell seeping out from under their closed doors. I'd messed up our schedules by getting switched into honors math last year and honors science this year. Now I save my breaks for when Gracie can get a pass, too. I found her with twenty minutes left before dismissal, switching locks between lockers in the eastern hallway when she should have been in art.

"I was worried you wouldn't make it," Gracie said.

"Told Mr. Craft I had diarrhea. He claimed you can't have it every day, and also that it doesn't take a half hour to go if you do, but I let out a well-timed fart and got the pass."

"He clearly has a different relationship with cheese than we do."

"Look at Locker 683. It is just dangling there," I said.

"Jennifer Plotkin," Gracie hissed as she made the switch.

"How do you know that?" I said.

"I can pay attention when it matters," Gracie said.

I was checking the locks at the end of the hallway when a flash of color caught my eye. I walked up to Ms. Bloom's science lab and pressed my face against the door's window.

Inside was a leather jacket with the collar turned up, shoulders broad, and a perfect fall of fabric. If the country of Italy were going to a party, this is the jacket it would pull on. And it was cream colored. The audacity. Not white, not beige, not eggshell. You could easily paint a spa with this color. And someone was wearing it to school. I didn't even know if that was legal.

"Come help me," Gracie said.

"Can't. Falling in love with some outerwear," I said.

"I want this sign, but I can't reach it. What is an academic bowl, anyway? Like a super-smart salad?"

The cream-colored jacket turned sideways. It was chock-full of Ethan Rogers, who I happened to be crushing on.

Not, like, tell-my-friends-and-strategize level of crush, but quietly-obsess-about-our-future-together-each-time-we-crossed-paths-and-then-immediately-forget-his-existence territory. A month ago, I was behind him in line at the cafeteria when he helped a fifth grader with some change. Being able to count and think of someone other than himself made Ethan one of our town's most eligible eighth graders.

But he'd been wearing a hideous windbreaker then.

"Gracie, come here. It's Ethan," I whispered. "He's so hot."

"He's mildly tepid."

"Look at what he's wearing."

Gracie stood on her tippy-toes and pulled herself up on the door. "Wow. I could see a two- to three-month relationship built around that jacket."

And then Ethan turned from his friend and looked right at us.

"He's looking at me. Or maybe he's looking at you," I said.

"How would he see me?" Gracie said from a thousand feet below. "What's he doing?"

"The corners of his mouth are going up. I can see his teeth."

"He's smiling at you!"

I dropped down to Gracie height and headed toward our lockers before I was tempted to smile back.

The final bell rang as we plodded to the Activities Room. Classroom doors flew open. Kids barreled into the hall, swinging backpacks and lunch totes. Girls drew together in chatty packs. Boys yelled and pushed. Teachers leaned against the walls, glancing at their watches and rolling their eyes at each other.

Everyone was about to be free. Or if they weren't free, it was by choice. But not us.

"Do we really have to do this?" I asked Gracie.

"Yes," she said, surprisingly firm. "The fact is, we can accomplish something. From the way everyone talks, it sounds like people are accomplishing things all the time. Exhausting, and we shouldn't have to hang with randos after school, but if we do, we'll make the best of it."

I shook off the chill that had been creeping after me all day. Everything could be okay. I hugged Gracie and said, "At least we're together. Now we just need this club to be even marginally chill and we'll be fine."

But when I pulled back, Gracie wasn't smiling. I'd never seen her look so shocked. Turning around, I saw why.

Standing at the front of the Activities Room, holding a clipboard and welcoming Community Action Club members inside, was Madison.

CHAPTER 6

WHEN THE BEST IDEAS COME FROM THE WORST PEOPLE

GRACIE

That afternoon, Salty Hour

I would have been less surprised to walk into a classroom full of cobras dancing to bad techno music than to find Madison leading the do-gooder group that was the key to my future.

She turned to us and jammed her clipboard into her hip. "Are you lost?"

I grabbed Helen's hand and said, "In a cosmic sense, yes. What are we doing here? What's next? Are we the only beings in the entire universe who eat spray-can cheese?"

Helen handed the envelope from Ms. Varone to Madison.

"We've been sentenced to save the world and heard this was the place to do it," Helen said.

With the clipboard tucked under one arm, Madison tore open the envelope. She scanned the letter, flipped it over, and back to the front again. Her perfect skin turned red around her neck and temples until she looked like a gorgeous gargoyle caught on fire. Then Madison folded the letter into a rectangle with razor edges, slid it into her skirt pocket, and led us into the Activities Room without another word.

Inside, the A Girls sprang into action from the front row of tables.

"Those are the losers who ruined our Cheerfest send-off," Ashley said.

"You can't let them in here," Avery pleaded.

Madison twisted her long rope of hair into the perfect blond topknot. You could see that she was thinking. I knew that from Helen. These brainiacs definitely have a look about them. People always say it looks like someone is constipated or trying to poop when they're thinking, but to me it looks much more like a *Did I just poop in my pants and does everyone know it?* This is one of the many advantages to being a feeler more than a thinker. You never look like poop is involved, even when it is.

"It's okay with me if they join," Isabella said, twirling her gorgeous glitter baton and giving us a little wave. "We won Cheerfest, and 'one spirit, one team, one win' should apply to everything in life, right?"

Madison positioned herself behind a podium at the front of the room. "Community Action Club is open to all members of the Darlington Middle School community, no matter how you got here."

"Not fair," Avery said, but Madison put up a hand.

"I have spoken. And we are in fact saving the world, so why doesn't everyone have a seat so we can get started."

Other than the Cheer coalition, it was an odd collection of kids: Isabella, who was in Cheer but not technically a Madison follower; Larisa, who was sort of new, but already running the debate team (shudder) and pleasantly ignored us when we sat together at lunch sometimes; some other smarties I didn't know very well; a few members of the geek squad, who carry duffel bags full of tech equipment everywhere they go; and some boys wearing sportsball shirts. And I got a complete surprise looking in the back row.

"Michael F., fancy meeting you here," I said.

He turned a scrumptious shade of purple and pushed out two chairs.

"What are you doing at this little soiree?" I asked.

"Shhhhh," he said like the adorbs librarian he was destined to be someday. "I've been in the club since fifth grade. We got the school to switch to reclaimed water for the front lawn sprinklers last year. Pretty cool."

There was no denying it. I was starting to get the eensiest crush on a dude who thought dirty water was in. This is why you should never listen to people who say Bigfoot isn't real or you can't wiggle your ears independently of each other. Anything is possible.

Madison banged a gavel on the podium. "I call our April meeting to order."

"Second," Larisa said.

"Third," I yelled.

Madison rolled her eyes. "We don't need a third. Would the secretary please read our mission statement?"

Michael F. cleared his throat and said, "This is a club for students, created by students, committed to nurturing education in our middle school community and creating positive change by convincing decision-makers to take action."

"Good job, Mr. Secretary," I whispered.

"It just means I take notes to share with the group," he said.

I didn't know if he was legit super cute or if his cuteness level was enhanced because he lived nearby and actually spoke to me, but his handwriting was excellent, so they were lucky to have him either way. Maybe this wouldn't be so bad! Helen and I could hang in the general zone of accomplishment without doing or saying anything, and I could chat with this potentially crushable boy.

But Helen seemed to have other ideas.

"You don't actually do anything?" she asked Madison. "You ask the grown-ups to do things. The action is by the adults, not the kids."

Madison ignored her. "We have two projects and a little more than a month left to get them done. I'm not leaving unfinished business for the seventh graders to lead. Let's make it happen. Where are we on Strawmageddon?"

Isabella bounced out of her seat and joined Madison at the podium.

"Our goal has been the total annihilation of straws on the middle school campus," Isabella explained. "I am psyched to share that the cafeteria has agreed to eliminate straws for the next fall semester and see how it goes!"

The room erupted in very gentle clapping.

"This was a total team effort," Madison said. "Each of you writing emails and attending school board meetings—as I instructed—made a difference."

"Is that like a cheese board?" I asked Michael F.

"More like the people who live in town elected to decide the school budget, which superintendent to hire, stuff like that," he whispered.

"We'll check straws off as an accomplishment, then?" Madison said.

Isabella looked less triumphant all of a sudden. Her baton picked up speed.

Madison stomped her foot. "Just say it. I won't be here next year to drag this stuff out of club members. What is the problem?"

"Well," Isabella said, "the principal said we can't ban people from bringing straws into school."

"Who are these devils buying plastic straws and bringing them into my school?" Madison said.

"Juice boxes come with straws," Isabella pointed out.

"Some people need a flexible straw for feeding issues, too."

Stop! Those words came out of my mouth. The mouth that had just decided it was time to keep quiet.

The entire room turned toward the back. Michael F. wrote furiously.

"What are you doing?" I asked him.

"It's a great point. I'm putting it in the notes," he said.

"Obviously we won't go after the kids who physically need straws, but everyone else gets peer pressure—" Madison started.

Ashley broke in. "Does that go for coconut water that comes with a straw attached, too? Because that is about hydration."

"Avery," Madison forged ahead, "make juice-box-size flyers with dead turtles as a warning. Anytime a kid drinks with a straw, we go up with a big smile and stick it to their juice box—or coconut water."

"I don't know if this is a great strategy for building community," Larisa said.

I didn't understand why Madison couldn't take getting rid of most of the bad thing, but that didn't seem to be the way she operated. Like if I was drinking a juice box—which I was now desperate for—and noticed other people weren't using straws, I might come to my own decision to stop. Not everyone needs to be terrified into doing the right thing. Sometimes you just need a little more info.

"Let's vote. All in favor of putting human feelings above the mass extinction of marine animals?" Madison said.

Helen shot her hand into the air. She was the only one.

"I thought you fell asleep," I whispered to Helen.

"I'm like 50% asleep, 25% thinking about whether it would be cool or creepy to get the same jacket as Ethan, and 12% listening," Helen said.

"What about the other 18%?"

"It is 13%, and you know I always leave 13% of my brain empty."

"You're so good at math. I wish we had popcorn," I said.

"I wish we had juice boxes," she said loud enough that the whole room turned to us again.

But then the lights dimmed. A projector dropped from the ceiling and two words appeared:

PERIOD EQUITY

Madison let them hang there in the room. I sat up in my seat. It felt like there was static electricity all around us and one movement could make a spark go off. There were a handful of groans and giggles and a lot of squirming. Madison didn't acknowledge any of it.

"This is the big one," she said. "With straws defeated, we can all focus on putting pads in every girls' bathroom at Darlington Middle School."

"Finally," Larisa said.

The Cheer girls gave a golf clap. Isabella threw her baton into the air. A new slide appeared on the screen.

"Pads and other period products are not luxuries," Madison went on. "They are basic healthcare that girls need to be safe. Not having them is a reason girls miss class. Studies show many struggle to afford them. Some states require schools to give out these products free of charge, but even in those places, they're not always stocked. Obviously, our state isn't one of them anyway. Everyone deserves period equity. It shouldn't matter where you live. And just because the government doesn't make us do it, doesn't mean we can't make it happen in Darlington."

A sportsball boy raised his hand. "I know you brought this up before—"

"At four meetings," Madison snapped. "We've been working on this for months, Jasper."

"Sure, but if things are really moving now, I mean—it's more of a girl thing than a school thing, so this isn't a club thing."

"Was your body grown in a uterus?" Madison asked, not waiting for an answer—which was good because Jasper looked totally confused. "Then you are here because of periods. In some cases, problem periods. It isn't a girls' issue. It is a human issue."

"Also, girls aren't the only ones who need pads. Anyone who menstruates uses them."

That was my voice. Again. What was I doing? Michael F. scribbled away.

"That doesn't even make sense," Jasper said.

I couldn't help myself. Truth coursed through my veins and spewed out of me.

"You can have a uterus and a period whether you are a girl or not," I said. "One is a very messy monthly biological phenomenon, and the other is a mash-up of my actual personhood with the little boxes society tries to cram us into. Ipso facto, I-uterus-therefore-I-bleed—you should throw a few pads in all the bathrooms to make sure everyone is included."

Helen put her fist out in front of me and you better believe I bumped it.

Madison growled lightly. "Makes sense. Very annoying coming from you, but I will update the handout, because we should include everyone who gets a period. And even kids who don't should get used to seeing pads."

And just like that we were skipping down the path to accomplishment because of me. Squee!

"Back to business," Madison said. "I met with a school board member when they happened to be on their morning run, and I happened to greet them with their preferred espresso beverage. Now we have an ally, and we're on the next meeting agenda. A week from Monday."

"This is a cool project, but I don't get what we would say in our letters," said one of the duffel bag boys. "If we're not a girl or someone with a period."

Michael F. stood up. From the way everyone spun around to look, I took it that this was not a typical thing.

"None of us are turtles, and we all spoke up for them with the straws. We can do that for pads," he said and then fell back in his chair like a one-ton weight.

My head was spinning. No one officially talked about periods at school, except in health. And even then, if anyone got real for a second, everyone laughed. Mommy threw me a period positivity party after my first time, and no one came. Not even Helen, because her mom freaked out, and that was back when Helen listened to her mom. If we could talk about pads at school, maybe we could talk about everything else that came with periods—like cramps, and when you just needed a break. I mean, I talked about my cramps all the time, but my personal comfort level didn't make much of a difference with no one listening. What Madison was saying could matter to how kids existed in our school. How I existed.

"How can we get this done?" I shouted.

Madison stared at me for a minute, looking genuinely shocked, but then addressed the group. "I'm giving you a handout with facts supporting this cause. We'll split them up now. Each of you will share your fact at the school board meeting or email them ahead of time—copy me—if you're not turtle enough to do it in person."

PERIOD EQUITY TALKING POINTS

- Girls ^ AND OTHER KIDS WHO MENSTRUATE ^
need maxi pads to attend class.
- Some kids with periods struggle to afford
maxi pads and other products.
- Kids as young as nine years old are getting their periods.
Access can't wait until high school.
- Many girls ^ AND OTHER KIDS ^ with periods have felt some shame,
stigma, or self-consciousness about their period.
- Pads in school bathrooms normalize periods and give access where
girls ^ AND OTHER STUDENTS ^ actually need them.

Helen finally opened her eyes.

"It won't work," she said.

"Excuse me?" Madison snarled.

"The board won't do this just because you give them a bunch of data."

"You're looking at a group of students who convinced them to eliminate straws next year."

"That was getting them to stop doing something," Helen said. "Plus, it saved them money, so that was getting them to stop doing two things."

"That doesn't even account for the impact on spitball fights," I said.

"Neither of you even go to school board meetings, so how would you know?" Madison said.

"I'm a certified expert in asking adults to spend money on things I need and being told no," Helen said. "Your little straw thing let the school stop stocking and spending. For the pads you're asking the school to start stocking and spending. It won't work. You need to go big."

"We should be sharing personal stories, from the heart, about what this all means," I offered.

"Barricade the bathrooms until they give in to our demands. I'm talking chaining ourselves to toilets, supergluing doors shut, calling every reporter in the area until the sky above the school is full of news choppers telling the world about these children who just want to bleed onto some quilted plastic. Better yet, we won't leave until they turn all the bathrooms into non-gendered single stalls." With that, Helen laid her head back down.

Everyone was quiet for a second, even Madison.

"Helen has a point on persuasion," Larisa said. "Obviously we shouldn't do a single one of those things—"

"All of them, you need to do all of them together," Helen yelled without lifting her head.

"—but this action may require a different approach than our other projects," Larisa said.

Madison seemed to snap back to herself then. "This is not up for discussion. Period equity will be my crowning achievement for middle school. Imagine me putting on my résumé that we accomplished in our school what real-life activists can't do in our state. I will make the presentation to the board on how they can implement this plan. All you people need to do is stand in support."

The ten-minute warning for the activities' bus came over the loudspeaker, and just like that the meeting was over. Michael F. promised to share his perfectly gorgeous notes with everyone over email. I slid my address over. He said that he had everyone's address already through the school directory, but he still took the paper, turned purple again, and shuffled out after everyone else. That left me, Helen, and Madison.

"Interesting and completely unexpected addition to the conversation, Gracie," Madison said, but she didn't wait for me to respond. "Anyway, as you saw, we're serious about this. I don't want you two screwing anything up. Let's make a deal."

"We're listening," Helen said.

"Stay out of this, and I'll tell Ms. Varone that you each actually did something. Then you can get out of loser jail and back to your regular loser existence," Madison said.

"It won't work. Which means we won't accomplish anything as our punishment requires. Madison, I'm sorry, but we have no choice. You'll find us chained to a toilet tomorrow wearing T-shirts that say, 'Community Action Club made me do it,'" Helen said.

"You're a nightmare, and I won't put up with it," Madison hissed.

"You're a mean girl, and I'm over it," Helen said.

My heart thumped against my chest so hard I couldn't stand it. I could deal with Principal Varone's irritation. And I was always up for a battle with our nemesis. But taking on both at once seemed exhausting. This was not the post-epic-prank chillfest I'd planned for.

"Tell Varone we helped accomplish the straw apocalypse and we'll stay out of this other thing," I offered.

Madison frowned. "We did that before you got here."

"What about the juice boxes? I'm sure we can make a few kids cry over their apple juice," I said.

"It would be my pleasure," Helen said.

"Fine, but no supergluing, chains, or anything else. Period equity matters," Madison said and turned her back on us.

In the hallway, I gave Helen a bear hug.

"I know this is weird, but I wanted to get involved in the period thing. You know, in that I-bleed-therefore-I-am kind of way," I said.

Helen sighed. "Trust me, I get it. But what they're planning will get a big fat nothing. We need an anything. Let the Reign of Juice Box Terror begin. Now, let's go find out if the activities' bus is somehow worse than the regular bus."

I felt a stomachache coming on, and not only because I had partaken in all-you-can-eat-spaghetti and a massive, under-cooked chocolate chip cookie for lunch, in what I had not even appreciated was to become a strawless cafeteria after we graduated. The period project mattered. I actually cared about it, even though I hadn't known of its existence an hour ago. On the other hand, Helen was right. Madison's plan probably wouldn't work. We were making the right choice not getting involved. I was almost completely sure of it.

CHAPTER 7

PERIOD.

HELEN

A week later, last period, aka oh, oh, you see what I did there

I was obliterating an algebra test when it happened. That feeling of nearly imperceptible damp on my derriere. I shifted in my seat, trying to convince myself it was just another case of swamp butt. I vowed to never wear fancy yoga pants to school again, even if they were my nicest clothes and I looked completely awesome in them. Gold lamé sweat wasn't worth it.

A few more problems in, I started to panic. The damp had turned to wetness. But that was impossible. Since I first got my period at eleven years old, my cycle averaged longer than twenty-eight days—you know I graphed those data points—and my last time was when Gracie and I were chalking the back wall of the Cruller Castle with donut graffiti. Only twenty days ago. I admit my distribution was still all over the place, but more than a week off was not expected.

Pencil down, I reached into my bag, searching the inner pockets. There had to be something in there. A pad, a tissue, an old sock . . . nothing. Well, something. A pamphlet from Sage Academy for Girls. *Found this in Mom's purse,* a pink sticky note said in my sister's demonic scrawl.

The universe was mocking me for rolling my eyes at Madison's period project. In the last week I'd fished some juice box straws out of the trash to deliver to her as tribute, but otherwise I'd put the caring nonsense out of my mind.

Madison and I had math together. I usually tried to avoid all human contact in class, but she was behind me, two rows back, two columns over.

I turned and whispered her name.

She picked her head up and gave me a death glare.

I mouthed, "TAMPON."

She lifted her shoulders.

I coughed, "Periodgggggghhhhhh."

"Enough, Ms. Wells," Mr. Craft said from the front of the room. "Eyes forward on your own paper."

Even for Mr. Craft it was a half-hearted admonition. He knew I didn't need to cheat. Still, now my only option was to fly through the test and run to the bathroom, hoping I would drop my pants to find a pool of sweat instead of what I knew was there.

I stacked my papers, threw my bag over my shoulder, and shuffled to the teacher's desk using my legs only from the knees down.

"I didn't hear a bell, did you, Ms. Wells?" Mr. Craft took my papers and pulled his red pen out of his pocket.

"No, but—" I said.

"Let's see how you did," he said and flipped through the pages. He put the pen down. It had taken a while to train him—at the beginning of the year I'd write arcane proofs I found in my mom's college textbooks whenever I got called to the board—but for the last few months we'd developed a truce where I would get every single question in class correct in exchange for him leaving me alone.

"You didn't show your work on the last three problems."

I took my test, slammed it down on his desk, and wrote out the dumb work using his dumb red pen.

Handing it back, I gave him my biggest, most terrifying smile. "I need to go to the bathroom."

"Have a seat and wait for the bell. You know the rule: No bathroom passes for the last ten minutes of class."

"It's diarrhea again, sir," I said, my face so plastic it hurt.

Mr. Craft reached into his center drawer and pulled out the wrong stack of passes.

"I don't need the nurse," I said.

"Ms. Shapiro is in our building today, and anyone who leaves class for diarrhea more than once a week needs the nurse," Mr. Craft said. He looked at his watch. "I'm calling her in three minutes to check that you made it."

I snatched the pass and backed out of the room.

In the hallway at last, I abandoned my knee-clenched walk. If my hips swinging released more blood, so be it. I planned to make a pit stop in the bathroom no matter what trouble it led to with the nurse. I was imagining how to engineer a temporary pad out of toilet paper when my path to the ladies' room was blocked—by Ms. Varone.

"You're not in this hallway at the end of the day," I blurted.

"How would you know that?" she said.

"It's my pooping bathroom, so I'll just—" The door was right there, but her hand was in front of it. I dropped my pass into her palm.

"This is a nurse's pass," she said.

"Mr. Craft is really committed to our bowel health, but I'll be fine if I pop a squat," I said.

Ms. Varone kept staring at me. I had no idea what she wanted to hear. I tried to let out a fart to make my case, but when it mattered most, I had nothing brewing.

I could have just told her I might have my period. But also, I couldn't. I cannot explain why it was easier for me to say poop, turd, diarrhea, dump, load, or any other phrase for a steaming pile than to talk to someone about my period when I didn't want to.

"I'll walk you to the nurse's office," Ms. Varone said.

It is possible that falling out of an airplane or jumping into hot lava could be worse, but having to walk alone with an adult you have nothing to say to has to be up there on the list of most abominable ways to spend your time. I started mentally reciting my favorite prime numbers to stop me from running through the plate glass windows and into the parking lot.

"You know, Helen—" Ms. Varone said as we rounded the last corner.

"Eight hundred seventy-seven," I said.

"Relationships evolve . . ."

The plate glass was looking more and more appealing.

"Have you told your friend you'll be in all honors classes next year? That things are changing for you in high school?" Ms. Varone's concerned tone was not helping.

"I have tons of time to screw that up. No need to stress Gracie out," I said.

"You will be close to lots of people in your life, different people at different times. It's important to recognize when someone might be holding you back," she said.

"I couldn't agree more, Ms. Varone. What if you get to the end of this life and the good relationships—the ones that were true—were all that mattered, and the honors classes and grades and everything else were the real distractions that only small-minded people focus on?"

Ms. Varone shook her head. "Helen, you're not the first student to lash out at me and you won't be the last, but you may be the one with the most to lose."

Luckily, we'd finally reached the nurse's office, and the principal opened the door for me. I slipped in before she could impart any more words of wisdom.

Unluckily, Ms. Shapiro had plenty to say.

"Here she is," she said into the phone. "I'll find out what took so long." She hung up and peered at me. "Helen, that was—"

"—Santa Claus."

"No, it was—"

"—the President?!"

"ItwasMr.Craftandhewantedtoknowwhereyouwere." Ms. Shapiro said it so fast that we both ended up laughing. "But seriously, girlie-girl, you cannot keep doing this. In the last month you've had enough loose stool to constitute dysentery, symptoms you clearly concocted to mimic ringworm—for which I have to say the makeup was impressive—and leprosy."

"Won't you be sorry when my nose falls off," I said, and went to plop down on the cot—but its gleaming white sheet stopped me.

"I have my period," I blurted out, but it sounded in my head like someone else had said it.

Ms. Shapiro nodded in the most relaxed way possible. She unlocked the supply cabinet and came back with a box.

"You could have told Mr. Craft," she said, handing it to me. "Even male staff members are trained in how to address these situations."

"But I shouldn't have to, right? I should be trusted to go to the bathroom. Anyway, I only need one, not the whole box."

"It is only one," she said.

Impossible. The box was nearly the size of a small paperback book. Thick cardboard shrink-wrapped in plastic. I opened it to find a pad surely meant for a horse or an elephant if they got periods.

"They're ridiculous and pretty expensive, but we get them from the same supply company as everything else," Ms. Shapiro explained. "I should keep a stash of regular pads in here for you girls, but I'm already spending my own money on extra bandages and the ice packs you never return."

"I wouldn't expect that," I said, still staring at the box. "I just . . . I did not account for sticking a small mattress in my crotch when I planned today's outfit."

"Do what you can with it, and then you stay here until final bell. If you want, we can call your mother," Ms. Shapiro said, writing me a bathroom pass.

I thanked her as I slipped out the door with zero plans to return. Being tormented at bus lineup for a bloodstain seemed the much lesser evil compared to Mom sitting me on a towel in the back seat while she lectured me on the personal responsibility inherent to feminine hygiene.

I made it back to the bathroom and flung myself into a stall. The heat building in my chest and cheeks finally made it to my eyes. I didn't bother to fight the tears anymore. They dropped silently in big wet blobs onto the tile floor as I bent over to slide down my pants. The damp, the wetness, even the drip had been very real, and it was all very red.

As if things couldn't have gotten any worse, the bathroom door opened and whatever monster came in picked the stall next to me. My fingers fumbled as I extricated the gigantic pad, dropping the box on the floor. I managed to peel off the mile-long plastic strip and was devising a way to try to clean myself and my clothes with the world's thinnest toilet paper when, all of a sudden, a tampon appeared from beneath the stall divider.

"Thank you," I whispered and grabbed it. "You are my fallopian fairy godmother."

A minute later, feeling almost like an actual human being, I came out of the stall and nearly lost it all over again.

"Madison?"

She stood at the mirror looking weird and pale, and like she might be the next one of us to cry.

"I thought you were being a jerk because you always finish way before the rest of us," she said, her voice tight. "But when I turned in my test, I heard Mr. Craft on the phone with the nurse and I realized what happened."

"You just saved me from an industrial-size pad that's used to soak up oil spills when it's not tackling teen periods." I twisted around so I could see my butt in the mirror and sighed. "But these pants never stood a chance."

"I'll change into my Cheer uniform so you can wear my shorts," Madison said.

She was being nice. Deeply weird.

And then we stood there. In silence. I timed my breathing to the flickering of a fly in the long fluorescent light above.

"You know I really care about period equity, right?" Madison said.

"Your crowning achievement, I heard. Can't your dad just buy you that résumé line?"

I hated how good it felt to say that. She didn't take the bait, though.

"I was home with my dad when I first got it. Totally caught me by surprise, even though I knew it was a possibility from a scientific perspective. He was working for a super-important client, so I just said I need some pads. I didn't want to make a big deal, and he said sure, let me go get you some. And then he comes out of his office and hands me a stack of legal pads."

I wanted to laugh but kept it in until Madison chuckled and rolled her eyes. And then I asked, genuinely curious, "What did you do?"

She lifted her hands. "I thanked him. I mean, it was some high-quality, pre-hole-punched stationery. And then I shoved a washcloth in my underwear and rode my bike to the pharmacy. When I got home, I set up an auto-delivery on products, and started filling those legal pads with period research. Do you understand I've been building to this project with everything else we've done with the club—the seasonal plantings, the used book drive, the reclaimed water initiative, Strawmageddon . . ."

Madison stopped and scrunched her face. "Do you hear screaming?"

We peeked out the bathroom door just as the yelling came closer.

"Helen! Helen!"

And in a flurry of flailing elbows and knees, Gracie whirred by, screaming my name.

"Get in here," I yelled back.

Her high-tops screeched to a stop and she ran backward into the bathroom, wearing a paper doll dress that crinkled as she hugged me.

"Are you having a fashion emergency?" she asked, panting.

"Yes! As are you!" I said and hugged her again.

"We were in art and out of nowhere I found myself making a paper dress. Ms. Despinos insisted we make fake Chihuly glass out of tissue paper, but I couldn't help myself. I ripped out massive reams of paper and Reggie lay on top so I could cut around him. Once it was done, I took my other dress off," Gracie said, handing me a wad of lime-green jersey knit dotted with neon-pink geometric patterns, "Reggie stapled this one over my jumpsuit, and

I ran. Because I knew you needed me. Or maybe I didn't actually know, but I had to find you."

"I always need you," I said. "I knew all our telepathy practice over winter break was not a waste of time."

Madison cleared her throat. "This is starting to get weird."

She was right. It was getting weird. The pants, the period, the home threats, the school threats, the mean girls, the jocks, the entire freaking world were all crushing me. I wanted to do something. That feeling may have been the weirdest thing of all.

"Madison, on the whole period-product thing—count us in," I said.

"Squeeeeee!" Gracie said.

But Madison snorted. "Now that you're personally affected, you're in? Or you just really want to chain yourself to a toilet?"

I still didn't think Madison's facts-and-figures approach would work. But I could admit that mine was a nonstarter, too. Gracie and I would have to figure something else out. Something big that no one could ignore and that would actually work. Maybe I couldn't do anything about the jocks or the honors track, but I could make sure no other kid in Darlington would have to use the couch-size maxi pads from the nurse's office, or worse, have no pad at all.

"Less chains, more school board meetings," I said, and I mostly meant it.

CHAPTER 8

SMALL CUTS CAN STING THE WORST

GRACIE

That night, Garlic Hour

Our house smelled like an unholy alliance of burnt garlic and weeping onion when I ran through the side door. I kicked off my shoes, jumped into my slippers, and flung my book bag to the top of the stairs. Mommy had a pot boiling, the oven blasting, and scraps of eggplants, onions, tomato, and garlic littering the kitchen counter. She was making my grandma's famous sauce for dinner, which meant I had to sneak some antacids to the table. But there was time. I had an hour before Helen and I were meeting to solve her period pants situation.

Mommy turned from the stove as I walked in. "I got an interesting email from the principal. She suggested you write an update on your punishment. Have you defeated the straws?"

"Is that a new pronunciation of 'hello'?" I said, gave her a kiss on the cheek, and tore into the bag of Pied du Fromage cheeses on the counter. Parmesan, Swiss, Ragusano, oh my!

"Can I keep these?" I asked, holding up a fontina wedge in one hand and Gruyère in the other.

"No, they're for tonight's dessert cheese board. But you can taste this." Mommy held out a spoonful of sauce.

Such a great mom and human. Such an awful cook. Still, I smacked my lips like always.

"Oh, yum, for sure. But pleeeeease on the cheese? The very first event of this summer's Cheesiad to celebrate mine and Helen's birthdays is Fondue Fumble! Two melting pots—one with fontina, the other Gruyère. We'll throw in chunks of bread from a foot away. The first to sink into the cheese loses. Or wins. I'm not sure, because even if you lose, you get to eat."

"Your birthdays aren't for a couple of months," Mommy said, handing me the Parmesan, the grater, and a bowl. I got to work shaving it as she added, "Besides, Mama and I thought maybe we'd celebrate yours with a little beach trip this year."

"I'll have to see if Helen can come," I said. "But I guess we can do the other events anywhere. 'Stink versus Stink.' You wear an eye mask. I hold something up to your nose. You guess whether it's a dirty sock or blue cheese."

"Might be more of a family trip," Mommy said.

"Right, and Helen is family. She came up with the Cheesiad finale. 'Which Whey Is the Pizza?' First, we make our own mozzarella. Then we make pizza with that mozzarella. Then I just assume we'll ascend to some higher plane of existence."

"We'll have to see what Mama says about all that," Mommy said.

Ugh.

I'm sharing groundbreaking cheese-based vacation plans, and one parent is waiting to form a united front to say no because they never tell you to wait for the other parent when the answer is yes.

When I finished helping with dinner, I headed into my Sugar Cabinet. Time to de-stress, and I had serious work to do anyway. Sugar, food coloring, shortening, fondant, icing paint, cupcake molds, marzipan, and sprinkles flew off the shelves and onto the island.

"If you were making an edible maxi pad, would you start with fondant or marzipan?" I asked.

Mommy gave me a look. "I'd stop eating sugar altogether and ask how I reached the point in my life where I was making edible maxi pads. Leave the cheese. Leave the sweets. Set the table."

I made a pile of plates, napkins, cups, and utensils and handed them to Mama as she walked into the kitchen.

"For me? You shouldn't have," she said, pushing them back. "No, really, you shouldn't have because you, my dear child, need to set the table."

Oh, I set the table all right. But I put everything backward. And upside down. Or as upside down as you can put something that is a circle.

"A cutlery rebellion," Mama said as we sat down to dinner.

"I suppose it's safer than a rebellion with cutlery," Mommy said.

I filled my plate with bucatini slathered in onion and butter tomato sauce and a side of sautéed eggplant dusted with Parmesan. Mommy tried to push a slice of bread onto me slathered with enough burnt garlic to slay an entire village of vampires. I didn't have the heart to tell her I couldn't eat it. The truth was I hated it—her Italian card could be taken away for crimes against garlic—but you don't crush someone's spirit like that when you can plead a pasta defense.

"I'm going for a bucatini belly instead. Anyway, Mama, if YOU"—I gave Mommy a second helping of side-eye—"were making a maxi pad to top a cupcake, would you use marzipan or fondant?"

Mama raised one eyebrow but didn't miss a beat. "Neither. Graham cracker dipped in white chocolate. Maybe a little royal-blue icing to pipe on a quilted pattern. But we need to discuss this email from school."

"We already are!" I told them about picking Strawmageddon just so we'd be done, then deciding to jump into the period project after Helen's pad disaster.

"I don't like you being so influenced by Helen and that girl who thinks you need to smell like disinfectant," Mama grumbled.

"Madison," I supplied. "But in this case, she's doing something awesome."

I told them all about the plan, how there was the chance this could change how you existed with a period at school, and that my contribution would be a Swag-n-Sweets table for the school board meeting.

Mommy and Mama gave each other that look that means they're about to lay into me. I wasn't having any of it.

"Before you tell me a cupcake can't change the world, gastro-diplomacy is a whole thing. I looked it up. You can totally win hearts and minds starting at the belly." I even tore off a piece of garlic bread and tucked in, deciding the heartburn later would be worth it to prove my point.

Mommy put her hand over mine. "You've never done anything like this before. Maybe we could have the cupcakes here, for fun, and then you can go and listen to the kids with more experience."

"What's more concerning to me is the Helen connection," Mama said.

"I know," I whispered, "she is an awful baker—everything ends up tasting like paste. Which is weird because you would think she'd be into the measuring and fractions, but don't worry, she can take care of the T-shirts."

Mama shook her head. "Let me be clear. It would be better if this were a project you were helping with on your own, instead of with Helen."

"I do everything with Helen," I said. And I was going to keep doing everything with Helen, so I didn't understand why we were even talking about this.

"And she gets you into trouble every time," Mama said.

I put down my fork. "Perhaps I get myself into trouble. Or do you think I'm not even capable of that? Maybe right now Helen's mom and dad are saying I get *her* into trouble."

"Sweetie, we've talked to them. Her parents also think Helen is the problem," Mommy said.

It felt like the floor was falling out from under me. I was starting to understand what Mommy meant about how we'd "have to see" for summer plans. The principal forcing us apart at school. Parentals pushing us apart at home. The chances of someone caring about what I wanted hovering around zero. I was capable. And I wanted to use my capabilities, even if I wasn't exactly sure what they were beyond making things delicious and adorable, on the period plan.

I pushed myself back from the table.

"One of you doesn't believe in me because I haven't done this before, and one of you doesn't believe in me because it involves my best friend. Perfect parenting," I said.

Mama's chair screeched on the floor. She followed me into the kitchen.

"I want to support you, Gracie. But your last endeavor with Helen ended with police sirens. It is wonderful you're passionate about something, but this house is strewn with half-finished projects that caught your eye and then got discarded—paintings, mosaics, crochet, a tree house without a roof. This one needs to count—it's going on your permanent record."

The fondant, the sugar, the color gels. I placed them all back into my Sugar Cabinet one by one, evenly spaced, facing forward. No one could say I had left any of this "strewn" about. You would think I was a slug oozing all over the house, leaving slime trails wherever I went.

And this didn't matter because of my permanent record. It mattered because it was important. I felt this period project very deeply, and not because I was embarrassed. I never tucked a tampon into my sleeve or tried to hide my butt.

Still, having a period was this extra thing you needed to deal with at school, and no one ever talked about all the problems it causes. Once a month I had to double over at my desk in cramps-induced pain, while it didn't even enter the conscious-ness of most boys.

I was still trying to find the words to explain why this all mattered. But how could we talk about anything real when my moms were bringing up crimes of half-finished tree houses from when I was seven?

"I have to go," I said, closing the Sugar Cabinet a little more forcefully than I normally would.

"Let's make our dessert cheeseboard and finish talking this out," Mommy called from the dining room.

"I'm picking Helen up—"

"After what I just told you?" Mama said.

"—and then we're going to Aunt Carmella's house," I said, turning back to the dining table to look at Mommy, know-ing that would get her good and she was a lot more gettable than Mama.

Mommy choked on her garlic bread. "Does my sister even know you're coming over this late?"

"Yes. And more importantly, Carmella knows we need to remove a stain of the great crimson wave from some gold lamé pants. Which sounds more biblical and more Broadway now that I've said it out loud than when it was in my head." Then I twirled out the door before either of them could respond.

I was so out of it on my march over to Helen's that I tumbled right into Michael F.'s tent. There were screams and cries inside and out. It felt like I was wrestling an alligator in a bad tracksuit.

"Death by nylon sheet!" I yelled as a flap covered my head.

71

"Gracie, stop moving," he called out from inside. "If you stand up and back, we'll be okay."

"Which way is Earth?" I cried, arms flailing.

"Down!" Michael F. yelled.

And sure enough, my feet found solid ground while I still faced into the tent. Then nylon pressed into my palms. There were warm hands behind it. They pushed and pushed until we both stood upright.

"Are you okay?" Michael F. asked me through the tent.

"Physically, I'm golden. Cosmically, the prognosis is bleak," I said.

The warm palms left mine, slowly, gently. Michael F. peeked his head out of a flap. "Come in out of the not-at-all cold."

I had never been inside a tent before. Sitting there on the ground while Michael F. rearranged the sticks and ropes that held the whole thing up, I was confident I had not missed anything.

"Did you get a vulture, or whatever comes before the dreaded condor?" I asked.

"Yeah, I think I finished my scouting requirements," he said and gave me the dorkiest little grin.

"Then why are you still out here?"

He stuck the last loose pole into the ground and sat on a little chair that wouldn't cut it as a footstool in most shoe stores.

"I kinda missed it," he said. "The first few nights I spent out here were stressful, because I was trying to tie knots and build a fire. But then I got used to the sounds of the neighborhood. My brain kept searching for them when I was back inside."

"Like a white noise machine, but with people shouting and car alarms?"

Michael F. nodded, then just stared at me. It was startling. Like, his eyes were so pretty behind those chunky glasses, but he didn't know how to use them around humans.

"Okay, well, I'm heading back into the real world," I said.

"Wait," he said, jumping up and hitting his head on the top of the tent. "I've got a thermos of hot chocolate, and I'm watching The Goonies tonight if you want to join me. It's this old movie about—"

"A bunch of kids who kick butt and find treasure. Yes, Michael F., I'm familiar with the flick, and I am seriously tempted. Alas, I have a date with destiny."

He put his hand on my arm as I lifted the tent flap. "Before, when you said you weren't cosmically okay, was it about falling, or something else?"

"Both," I admitted, "although a few minutes in here has oddly made everything better." I paused, feeling the warmth of his hand on my arm. "Hey, real talk?" He nodded, so I went on. "Do you think I can help with the maxi pad project? Like me, specifically, as a person?"

Michael F. used his free hand to push his glasses up way past where any nose could hold them.

"Yeah, I mean, if you follow Madison's lead and be a little more . . . I guess I would say a little less like yourself?" he said.

I peeled his fingers off my forearm. They were starting to feel clammy.

"I don't mean that in a bad way," he added. "You're just this full-of-life person, and the school board stuff is basically the exact opposite of that."

"I'm disappointing everyone tonight in new and exciting ways. This is why real friends matter. You know exactly how they'll disappoint you and how you'll disappoint them."

Michael F.'s giant eyes got even bigger. "So we're not real friends?"

"I don't know. You invite me to watch my fave '80s movie and drink sweets, and I want to kiss you. You tell me I shouldn't be myself like I have some other self in my glitter mini-backpack, and I want to make you vomit."

And with that, I popped myself out of the tent and ran the rest of the way to Helen's window before anyone else could say a bad thing to me.

"Be nice to me because I can't take another dramatic exit tonight. Take my temperature," I said at her window.

She reached out from inside her room to feel my forehead.

"You feel downright Shakespearean. If you get to Hallmark movie, I will take you to the hospital. What horrors have you been exiting anyway?" Helen said.

I gave her the skinny on my moms and Michael F.

Helen snorted. "They got it backward, Gracie. You need to be more you to make a difference. Creative, loving, unpredictable, and heart to the max. Big and then bigger."

"Hello! Thank you. We can totally use what is unique and

special about ourselves to change things," I said and slouched down onto the grass.

"I couldn't agree more," Helen said and leaned back to grab a long tube from her desk. She unfurled a massive piece of paper on the windowsill showing a map of the library.

"Oh, you're the 'big difference' crew now?" said a voice in the twilight.

"Somebody needs to put a bell on you," I said to Helen's little sister, Seraphine, once I finished screaming. I couldn't complain too much, though. The terror was refreshing.

"What's with the schematic?" Seraphine said, pushing me aside.

"It is a map, tiny baby," I said, elbowing her right back.

"Somebody needs to buy you a thesaurus," Seraphine said.

"Go to bed before I tell Mom you snuck out," Helen said.

"I'll tell her you're destroying the library," Seraphine said.

Helen rolled her eyes. "Please. I'm only going to make it look like blood is running down the walls."

Seraphine and I moved in closer.

"See," Helen said in full mastermind mode, "the school board meets in the middle school library. I pulled enough pictures off the superintendent's thirsty social media feeds to create this map.

"Look at how they set up the long U-shaped table where the board members sit. The wall behind it has three vents at the top. We get into the HVAC system, crawl to those vents, and set up red paint cans perched on levers, which are in turn connected to timers. As Madison is giving her facts-and-figures speech that no one will care about, we set off the timer, the levers go up, and blood, or, you know, red paint, comes streaming down the walls behind them. Who could ignore that?"

"Like the school is a person and the library is the womb," Seraphine said.

"Whoa," I said, searching her little face in the dark.

"I wasn't even going there, but you are totally right. What is happening in that tiny brain of yours?" Helen said.

"It is planning the best way to tell Mom," Seraphine said.

Helen gripped the windowsill and leaned out until her nose touched Seraphine's.

"Then I'll tell how you never gave back Mr. Wigglesworth. What did you do with him, anyway?" Helen said.

Seraphine ignored this and said, "Give me your narwhal dressed like a mermaid if you want me to keep quiet."

"Try getting your own life and leaving mine alone," Helen said.

Seraphine looked ready to launch another attack, but then she growled, turned, and walked off into the dark without another word.

"She's so smart," Helen said. "If she wasn't evil, I would totally ask her to join us."

"Demonic siblings aside, I wonder if this is too big," I said.

"No such thing," Helen said, rolling up the map.

"Also, too much like the 'vandalism' Varone is already mad about? Let's chat about a cupcake strategy and T-shirt plan to open some minds and win some hearts. Maybe some corsages made of tampons? We could dip them in school colors to really drive the point home," I said.

"Not cool to use the products for crafts that we need the school to pay for," Helen said.

"Excuse me, but you are a genius who should rule the universe. Cupcakes will be enough. Imagine: red velvet cake with a strawberry jam center, coated with strawberry whipped frosting, and topped with a marzipan maxi pad." I felt a sugar rush just describing it.

"I love everything about that," Helen said, "but that's your special skill set. Timed bloodlike substances flowing down walls without an apparent human cause is more me. Or us, I mean."

I opened my mouth to argue more, but honestly wasn't sure what to say. Helen and I never argued about anything. But if Madison's spreadsheets weren't the way to go, a red paint catastrophe in the other direction wasn't much better.

We were only separated by her windowsill, but I suddenly felt so far away from Helen. I wondered if she knew our parents were talking, but I didn't want to make her worry. The whole thing was too weird for words, so I found just enough to keep us moving.

"I was thinking you could apply your graphic design skills to the T-shirts we wear at the school board meeting?" I said. "Very much your thing."

"I can do that."

"Great. Let's table fake blood talk while we deal with the real thing. Now grab your shiny pants. Aunt Carmella is our only hope!"

CHAPTER 9

STAINS

HELEN

*That night, aka out late enough to avoid getting
yelled at for being out too late*

Carmella's old Victorian house was nothing like the rest of the Capes, bi-levels, and garden apartments in Darlington. It stood at the end of a long, winding driveway, its slanted porches and crumbling turrets protected by an army of overgrown rose-bushes and a swarm of squawking peacocks that could not have been strictly legal. Not the kind of place you'd wander up to. I assumed Gracie's aunt liked it that way.

I rang the bell. Twice.

Gracie groaned. "Is she seriously not home? On the last photo she posted, I commented, 'There will be blood at your house,' with eight owl and one pants emoji. Carmella gave it a heart. That's a binding contract."

I only really knew Carmella from her job at our town's pharmacy. She had a gray streak that made it look like she could conjure lightning and definitely decipher Gracie's emoji summoning.

I rang the bell again. "This place is deliciously creepy. We should hang here more."

"Mommy 'prefers' I don't come over without her—she only agreed to us all following each other on socials this year—but she leaves the 'decision' to my 'judgment,'" Gracie said.

"Only for the things they don't want to be tagged with," I said.

Suddenly we heard stilettos clacking inside. A dead bolt turned. A chair dropped. The door swung open.

Carmella kicked off her four-inch heels and pulled out her pearl earrings, then sorted through a stack of mail, all while never taking her eyes off us.

"Finally," she said and walked back into the house without another word.

"Do we follow?" I whispered.

Gracie rolled her eyes, took my hand, and led us inside.

While Carmella swapped her pharmacist jacket for a floral housecoat, Gracie and I set the table and then waited quietly in the kitchen. I searched for a cauldron, a mortar and pestle, something witchy, but everything seemed normal.

Carmella laid out macaroni and meatballs, stromboli with broccoli, and peach-glazed spareribs on the table. They were all just there. In her refrigerator. Cooked. I shoved it in my face because it was delicious and I hadn't eaten since lunch. Plus, it was weird for someone to have all this food ready to eat without calling a delivery place.

Then she sat down and poured us three cups of lemony tea.

"Mangia, gioia, you are skin and bones," she said, pinching Gracie's cheeks.

"Moms fed me. Not hungry," Gracie said.

Carmella leaned over and smelled her hair.

"My sister is into the garlic again. No surprise you didn't eat. You're a terrible liar, kid. Thank God for that, because there's nothing worse than a liar. Plus, it's not so easy. Il bugiardo deve avere buona memoria."

"I know," Gracie said, "a liar has to have a good memory."

"Good girl. Your mother continues her atrocities against the noble bulb, but at least she finally came to her senses and sent you to make the peace. You came. You're a brave girl. I respect that. And I accept. We can have the peace."

"No, Aunt Carmella, Mommy didn't send me. She doesn't remember what you all are fighting over, but I don't know if she'll ever want the peace."

"You wrote 'there will be blood' on my Instagram. Blood is family. I thought—"

"I'm here not as your niece, but as a client. The blood means actual blood. And I would prefer some buffalo mozzarella to all these meatballs, which I am sure you have."

Carmella slammed her mug on the table, rose slowly from her chair, and took Gracie's face in both of her hands. I was so nervous the buttered roll I'd shoved in my mouth fell back into my hand.

Then Carmella let out a big laugh and said, "Of course you do!" She kissed Gracie all over her head. "In a nice caprese salad—with the first basil from the garden—and then we'll go to the lab and you'll tell me all about your problem. Our blood feud will have to wait."

I was Wrong with a side of Wronger on there being a cauldron. After dinner, Carmella led us through what I figured was her back porch door, but actually connected to a lab that looked like a Sunday night crime drama was filmed there.

"Can I steal some beakers?" Gracie said as we sat side by side at a metal table.

Carmella tapped on a keyboard. "Take the 10 mL. I know you like eensie things. Now, clients! What are we doing? I've digitized my library so I'm not wading in ten thousand books for every question. You're trying to grow your hair like a horse? A big test coming up? Making someone fall in love with you?"

I gasped. "Aren't love spells super dangerous?"

"Only for the tourists. But of course, I'm joking. You can bumble through love like the rest of us."

Gracie handed Carmella my pants. Part of me wanted to melt into the earth never to be seen again over giving someone my stained clothes. If Gracie hadn't told me to save them, I would have shoved those leggings into a garbage bin on the other side of town before my mom ever saw them in the laundry. But I also felt in my heart like Carmella wouldn't judge me.

"You need a laundress, not an herbalist," Carmella said, pulling on a pair of gloves.

"They're lamé," I whispered.

"Lamé? In that case, get twelve exceptionally ripe tomatoes, the rubies of the garden. A tablespoon of cane sugar. Garlic—"

"Carmella, that's your marinara recipe!" Gracie yelled.

"I can't fix these pants, but at least you'll eat good." Carmella laughed, but we didn't. "Excuse me, but you're not upset just about the pants, are you?"

Gracie told her everything, from the stink blubs to the caring

project to making a paper dress to her maxi-pad cupcake suprem-
acy. I had never heard her so excited before, and this was a girl
who sang when the sun peeked through on a cloudy day and
danced when she had exact change at a store.

When it was all out there, Carmella sat back on her stool and
nodded.

"First of all, warn me in advance before you ever hand me one
of those cupcakes," she said. "But I support you. This is so important. And you'll see the effects right before your eyes. When is
the board meeting?"

"Monday night. We need to be there at 8:00 p.m.," Gracie said.

"I'll see you then," Carmella said.

"I didn't mean 'we' as in 'you.' I meant the galactic 'we,'"
Gracie said.

"My little love, your aunt happens to be one of those people
that boards in this town pay attention to, even if they don't like
what I say or do what I ask. Plus, they'll get nervous when they
see me, and that brings me joy. I'll say, 'I'm a taxpayer, and I support this.' They eat that stuff up." Carmella turned back to the
pants. "Now, let me see. With its metallic strands, how different
can lamé be from a tapestry?"

She mixed powders from vials and liquids from cold beakers
together in a big bowl, added a carafe of fresh water, and dunked
my pants in.

Gracie looked at me in a panic. "But Carmella, you don't
have to go—"

"You said that already, but you people only come here when

you need me. Even if you don't know it yet, you need me at this meeting. Helen," she said, "you see Gracie's mother's neck? Not my sister who doesn't talk to me, but Gracie's Mama. Perfect skin. That was me. She comes for beauty treatments, you come to conjure the laundry—no one comes to make the peace."

"Couldn't you apologize, Aunt Carmella?" Gracie said.

"For what?"

"For whatever you're fighting about."

"I don't remember. Does your mother?"

"No. I told you."

"It was too many years ago. All I know for sure was that it involved a pizzelle and that it was her fault," Carmella said.

"Is that like a pistol?" I whispered.

"Closer to a cookie," Gracie said.

"And besides," Carmella went on, stirring my pants in the bowl with a massive glass ladle, "sometimes arguments are really about what you're fighting over and sometimes they're about things broken for so long they can't be put together again. In any event, for this meeting, arm yourself with fennel in case you need to ward off any evil spirits."

"I feel like that is a car part, like check if the fennel is leaking," Gracie said.

"Or clothes. I hate when my fennel cuts into my armpits," I said.

"It is a vegetable. You'll find it in your kitchen. Well, not your kitchens. Take it from my counter when you leave."

Carmella took a fluffy towel out of a drawer and used it to wring out my leggings.

I couldn't believe it. The stain was gone.

"How?" I asked, running my hands over the flawless gold fabric.

"It is along the lines of a medieval stain buster. Was this your first period? Is that why you didn't have something? Talk to your mother," Carmella said, washing her hands.

"It was my twenty-second time," I said, "but it was early. Or maybe it was a late double take. I'm not sure, but the internet says it can take a few years for your cycle to even out."

"This may be one of the few times the internet is right, but your mother—" Carmella began.

"Doesn't talk about this stuff," I said.

Carmella pursed her lips, but in a sympathetic way. "Mothers sometimes have a way of surprising you. Or sometimes they're truly terrible."

"She's not terrible. But we're a thousand miles apart," I explained.

Carmella laughed. "Gracielle, can you imagine not dissecting every bodily function with Mommy?"

"No, but maybe there's a happy medium between everyone in each other's business and not speaking at all," Gracie said.

"Mommy will have to tell you her own story, but when I first got my period, we had an olive oil cake to celebrate the blessing and lament the curse," Carmella said.

"Here we go," Gracie said.

"We were at the produce stand. I was making a strong case against Brussels sprouts when I felt my mother slip something plastic into my hand. She told me, 'I love you, I'm sorry you're no longer a child, but it eventually had to happen.' I was confused, but I knew enough to go to the bathroom. I'd ruined my favorite Levi's that I'd spent two months of babysitting wages on—don't ever come to me with denim stains—and we had Brussels sprouts anyway."

"I don't believe in all this curse and loss of innocence stuff. I'm the same person I was before I had my period," Gracie said.

"I agree with you," Carmella said. "I am the same person, even now that my period has stopped. But that is a discussion for another day."

And with that she folded up my leggings, handed them back, and pushed us out of the lab and into the kitchen. "Helen, good luck with your mama. You're welcome here anytime."

Then she kissed Gracie on the forehead. "You, I love you, you have a gift. This is the year I teach you how to remove the evil eye on Christmas Eve. In the meantime, I will be your friendly neighborhood taxpayer at the school board meeting. Don't forget to tell your mother she's still dead to me. Ciao ciao!"

CHAPTER 10

SURPRISES

HELEN

Monday night, aka time for extra school

The night of the school board meeting started with dinner at the family table as usual. Mom behind her newspaper. Dad scrolling through reams of data on his phone. Seraphine bopping with her tablet and headphones. Plates full of pizza crusts and garlic knot crumbs.

I once read that *set* is the English word with the most meanings, but spend five minutes in my house and you would be sure it's the word *fine*. It had been uttered fifty times in fifty different ways that night, and now everyone was resigned to silence. Until I broke it.

"Scheduling note: I'm going out tonight," I said.

"Through the front door?" Dad asked without looking up.

"To the school board meeting," I said.

Mom snapped her paper to the next page. "For caring club?"

"Yes, ma'am," I said and got up to clear the table.

Mom put her hand on mine as I took her plate.

"Do you need me to be there?" she asked.

Well, that was unexpected. I honestly couldn't think of the last time Mom came to a school activity. I wasn't sure how I wanted to respond, but it wasn't exactly a no.

"Cool, I'm sure they care more about what you have to say," I said.

"I meant to keep an eye on you," she said.

"It's fine." I ran the crusts down the garbage disposal.

All weekend I'd stewed on what Carmella had said about giving my mom a chance to surprise me. I wasn't joking about her not being terrible. It's just that she wanted me to check off all these boxes at school and in life, and I wanted to pulverize the boxes into pulp.

Still, I'd promised Carmella I would try. I don't know the ramifications of lying to a witch, even if she was technically an herbalist who sometimes argues with dead people.

I took a deep breath. Then I set out the dessert bowls.

"The project is about periods, which is especially relevant to me right now," I said.

That got their attention.

"Not in front of your sister," Dad said.

I leaned over Seraphine while I dished out the ice cream. She was watching craft videos. I could hear the squeal of other children's joy through her headphones. They refused to get me a phone until high school, but the tablet was for her education. I guess her PhD will be in making unicorn poop slime.

"The Tiny Terror is in her own world. Also, she knows I get it. Why can't she hear? She will get it one day, too."

"We will cross that bridge when we come to it. Now, what does a caring club have to do with . . . *menstruation*?" Mom said it like the word was being pulled through her teeth by force. "What happened to straws?"

"It is Community Action Club. They're trying to get pads in the bathrooms so if you get your period, you always have something, whether it's your first time, or you don't have the money to buy your own, or you weren't expecting it," I said.

"A matter of equity," Dad said.

I spit out my Rocky Road. He was listening to me, and he got it.

"I support that," he continued. "Glad to hear it, Helen."

Now, Carmella probably envisioned me having this talk with Mom, snuggled on the couch over mugs of hot cocoa. Or maybe Dad finding me having a sad and asking, "What's up, champ?" Or maybe everyone all up in each other's business like Gracie's family where you know what they ate last night and how they pooped it out the next morning. But this was as close as we got to a heart-to-heart at Chez Wells, so I went for it.

"An equitable basket of products would have helped me when I started bleeding unexpectedly on Friday," I said.

Dad looked back and forth from me to Mom, then finally settled on her.

"Brenda, haven't you covered this?" he said.

"I did. Sweetie, I bought an extra box of supplies two months ago when they were on sale. You're out already?" she said.

It was now or never. To get real with them about what was happening with me.

"This time it was a week early," I said.

Seraphine's seat squeaked as she shifted from side to side.

My parents ducked down in their seats like they were hiding from something.

"Are you sure it was your you-know-what?" Mom whispered.

"I mean, it's been blood coming out of my—" I said.

Dad interrupted. "Couldn't this lady talk be taken to the bathroom? Or maybe it's more of an outdoor conversation?"

"Talk of period blood can't be confined within the walls of our house?" I said.

"Like the period blood you're going to send down the library walls?"

The voice was tiny, precise, and demonic. Seraphine never even looked up from her video.

"What?" Mom and Dad said in unison.

"Oh, sorry, you're all so loud I can't hear my program," she said with the world's sweetest smile. "I thought you were talking about how Helen and Gracie are making the library bleed tonight. Helen drew a picture of it in her room."

Mom wailed. Dad yelled. Chairs screeched.

"You were listening?!" I hissed at Seraphine. "But I heard the sound from your video."

"I can tell from the air in the room when it is time to listen. You never know when I'll turn the volume down," she said. "Should have given me the narwhal stuffie when I asked."

"The joke is on you because I threw the schematic out," I said.

But then Dad came back in the kitchen, holding the library map I'd drawn, complete with a legend for fake blood, levers, and timers. Only it was smeared in curry and peanut sauce and other things from yesterday's garbage.

"Care to explain?" Mom said.

"It was only a joke," I said.

"There are flow rate calculations," Dad said, removing a piece of lettuce.

I jumped up from the table. "I have to go. And I don't have any buckets of paint or blood or anything else, just some T-shirts I made to get the message out," I said, grabbing my bag and heading for the door—but then I felt Mom's hand on my shoulder.

"Don't bother," she said. Her eyes were wild, like she saw something she didn't recognize or understand. "It doesn't matter what you do with that club. You can't stay in this school system. We have to find a high school that can deal with you."

"You're the parents, you're supposed to be able to deal with me," I said.

"Let's all hold on," Dad tried, but she waved him off. Even Seraphine hopped down from her chair and was pulling on Mom's pant leg.

"I mean it, Helen," Mom said.

"I'm sure you do," I said. "We have to budget for an extra box of maxi pads when they're on sale, but you can afford some kind of private school?"

"If that's what it takes, we will make the sacrifice. You are a brilliant girl. You have to know how much trouble you're in. What if the school had pressed charges for your last prank?"

"They didn't," I said, hoping I could keep my voice steady long enough to get out of there.

"What if we had to pay for those bleachers?" Mom said.

"What if! What if! What if I walk out of this house and never come back? What if I send myself away, to save you the trouble?"

I didn't know what to say next. My chest hurt too much to go on. I thought about staying to talk to her. To all of them. For a split second, I imagined us sitting back down at the table to figure it out, for real. Not the end game or even any solutions, but how to exist in each other's lives. I knew none of that would happen, though. Besides, my hand was already turning the doorknob, and it felt like freedom.

My sneakers hit the pavement. The warm night air filled my lungs. I leaned into my churning legs. The more backyards I cut through, hedges I hopped, streetlights I spun around, the more it felt like vines that had been growing over me were dropping from my shoulders. I thought about running right past the school, to the edge of town, and what it would mean to never stop, and how bad it would be for Gracie if I really did, and if it would suit my parents just as well as sending me to Sage Academy to be fixed.

Then I ran right into the world's most gorgeous cream-colored leather jacket that was still chock-full of Ethan Rogers.

There was no stopping us from falling, but I would not let a grass stain come between us. I threw my arms around Ethan and rolled as we fell onto the middle school soccer field. The wind was knocked out of me, but my head was cradled by the soft turf. I opened my eyes to see Ethan's sapphire-blue eyes piercing my soul. He had to curl his eyelashes. I didn't even know any girls who had lashes like that. And he smelled good. Or maybe that was the freshly cut grass. But he definitely looked good, and how long had we been lying there without moving or saying anything?

Then his lips parted. "Hey."

"Is your jacket okay?" I asked, still trying to catch my breath.

"I guess. Are you okay?" Ethan said.

"I'm fine," I said.

He was still staring down at me. I thought I might melt into the turf.

"I never noticed that you have the tiniest freckles dancing in a line across your nose," he said and reached out with his index finger until it nearly touched my face.

That was too much. I pushed Ethan off me and inspected his arms and back. No green. No dirt. There was still a chance for us. The only explanation for caring more about me than that jacket and noticing my freckles of all things was a head injury. I ran my fingers through his hair. No blood. No bumps.

Then he reached his hand toward me again. I grabbed it right before he touched my hair.

He laughed. "You've got some grass in it."

He tried again. I swatted that down, too.

"But you touched my hair?" Ethan said.

"That was medical," I said.

He would need some instruction before we earned matching PhDs in applied mathematics and considered whether we believed in marriage and bought a two-family house with Gracie. I didn't plan to take a man's name, but *Helen Rogers* danced off my tongue and into that spring air.

"Ethan Wells," he responded.

"What?" I said.

"Aren't we playing a name-switching game?"

Maybe matching master's degrees.

He pulled me up to my feet.

"What were you running from anyway?" he asked.

"To school of all places," I said.

"Board meeting. Solid. Me too," he said.

"You're advocating for period equity?" I said.

He started walking toward the building and motioned with his shoulder for me to follow.

"I'm getting a plaque for being awesome at lacrosse, but my dad is on the school board so can't he give it to me at home? Anyway, I'll do a period thing while I'm there."

He said the word like a normal person, not as if he was spitting out gristle. I stopped and unzipped my sweatshirt to show off my homemade T-shirt: cartoon uterus in pink paint, one ovary holding a PERIOD EQUITY NOW sign, the other giving a thumbs-up, all on an old yoga top Gracie had snagged from her moms' to-donate bin.

"'Cuterus Uterus,'" Ethan read. "I like it. I didn't know you were good at art. Whenever I think about you, I think, like, math. But mean math."

"That is my brand," I said to my immediate regret because it sounded like a Mom Joke, but it was better than what was going on in my brain: an alert banner snaking through my cerebellum screaming, ETHAN ROGERS THINKS ABOUT ME.

"Do you have another one?" he asked.

I had ten more shirts in my bag. Ethan handed me his jacket as he pulled one over his jersey.

"Your jacket is awesome, by the way," I said and maybe held on to it a little too long.

"I know."

"Are you wearing the T-shirt to help us for real, or to be edgy?"

"I sort of like that you picture a cartoon uterus making me edgy. Hmm, what does this girl see as my starting point, but yeah, maybe it's both . . . Anyway, a few of us are donuting at the Cruller Castle after the plaques. It would be cool if you came with. I mean, you could invite the rest of the Cuterus Uterus crew if you want," he said.

Was Ethan Rogers's leather jacket asking me out for pastries on a school night? I was about to ask him to repeat himself to be sure. But then I heard shouting in the distance. Like bleed-free-or-die and give-me-super-absorbency-or-give-me-death kind of shouting.

"Sorry, Ethan Rogers and your jacket, but my bullhorn calleth."

CHAPTER 11

MAYBE BLEEDING WALLS WAS THE WAY TO GO

GRACIE

Monday night, Jam Hour

It is super important to create a fun atmosphere when you're trying to get people on your side. That is why I set up a sidewalk card table for the school board meeting decorated with every piece of pink and red paper I could find.

An air of exclusivity is also key. People like to think they're getting the last of something, so I didn't throw all my swag on the table at once. A glow stick from Halloween here, a pad of pink sticky notes there, and a handful of heart-shaped lollipops. I had the bubble machine going full blast and my travel karaoke set primed with both Beyoncé and Cyndi Lauper.

All that was missing was my amazing best friend with the T-shirts, plus the maxi-pad cupcakes, which I was saving for the board members.

A woman took one of my flyers on her way into the building. I wrote what I'd learned from Madison in words actual humans use and added a lot more neon and sparkly embellishments.

A GLITTER GUIDE TO PERIOD EQUITY

* Periods aren't a "girl issue"—they're a human rights issue.
* Pads are needed for school—we shouldn't have to choose between soaking in our blood and jetting home when our period arrives.
* Put pads in the bathrooms—we don't go to the bathroom in the nurse's office. The pads should be where we actually use them. Hint: It is also where we poop, so that's where you put the TP.
* Put pads in ALL the bathrooms—if a kid has a uterus, they may be getting their period no matter which bathroom they use.
* Seeing pads reminds people our periods exist. If we can get past that absolute minimum point, maybe we can talk about real equity, like what it takes to get through my period cramps and stay at my desk.

"Is this the meeting agenda?" the woman asked.

"That sounds super severe. I think of it more as a womb liberation concept board," I said.

She looked at me, confused, then leaned in. "Dear, you might want to use a tissue on your eyelids. Something's smudged—or maybe it's pinkeye."

"It is pinkeye, but the only thing contagious is my enthusiasm. See, I drew tiny glitterati uteruses on my lids with liquid black eyeliner and Punk Pink matte shadow. You are the first person to notice, so thank you," I said. When she went inside, I knew we had someone on Team Tampon.

Isabella and Larisa came by next.

"Gracie, this is amazing," Isabella said, her baton in motion as always. "Way to bring a public party to a public meeting."

Larisa looked like she might vomit. "Does Madison know you're doing this?"

"The real question is, which of you amazing girls will turn Cyndi Lauper's 'Girls Just Want to Have Fun' into 'FUNdamental rights' on the karaoke right now?"

Isabella took the mic, but Larisa grabbed it and gave it right back.

Finally, Helen appeared, throwing her bag on the table. "Hello fellow do-gooders."

I threw my arms around her. "First of all, ahhhh! I'm so happy to see you. Second, the shirt is even cuter now that the puffy paint is dry."

I immediately put one on and took a selfie of us kicking butt before we even walked into the building.

"We made a bunch," Helen said to the other girls. Larisa shook her head, but Isabella put one on while I twirled her baton as best I could.

"It looks like we're on a team!" she said.

"Is this it?" came a growl from behind us.

Madison. She wore a gorgeous black skirt suit with a white silk blouse. Her hair was set in a perfect French twist. It was like someone had put a lawyer in a miniaturizer and spit her out in the direction of the school. She even had a rolling brief-case that I immediately coveted for my karaoke supplies.

"Hello to you, too," Helen said.

"I'm shocked you're here and didn't burn down the school instead," Madison said.

"The night is young," Helen said.

I handed Madison a T-shirt. She leaned back like it was radio-active. "Do you see how I'm dressed?" she said.

"Like you're going to a funeral?" Helen said.

Michael F. joined us. He grabbed the T-shirt and put it on over his collared shirt and tie.

"Team Justice," he said and pumped his adorable fist into the air.

Madison pulled us all to the side as more parents and whoever else goes to these things went in.

"I wish there were more of us," she said. "I can't believe the A Girls didn't show, and, like, none of the boys."

We all looked at Michael F., but he shrugged as Madison kept yapping.

"The meeting starts in five minutes. We need to get inside, write our names down on the list of speakers, take our seats, and not do anything bizarre that might tank the project. I'll give the presentation when the club is called on the agenda, and you each say something supportive. Club-approved talking points only or I will tackle you. Any questions?"

I shot up my hand.

"When is the pastry portion of the meeting?"

•   •   •

Inside, the library had been transformed into the saddest ever wedding hall. There was a U-shaped banquet table draped with tablecloths in our school colors. Everything was plastered with screaming versions of our badger mascot. In the middle of the U was a podium and microphone and rows of folding chairs. Maybe it was less wedding and more boring Renaissance festival performance.

Madison and the others took seats in the front row. There is no helping some people. Helen saved me a seat behind them while I handed out my maxi-pad cupcakes to the board members.

"Aren't these interesting," said a woman in red-and-black plaid pants.

I added the extras to the buffet behind the tables and reached to grab a handful of chicken wings. How bad could a government meeting be if it involved snacks?

"Those are for school board members only," a grumbly dude said next to me.

"But I'm a school student, so what's a wing between ruler and subject?"

He started muttering again so I backed off—and straight into Aunt Carmella.

"You actually came?"

She shoved cylinders of foil into my hands. "No, I'm a mirage. And those are not chicken cutlet sandwiches for you and your tall, sullen friend. And you," she said, pushing me back and taking the entire bowl of wings while glaring at the grumbly man, "my tax dollars pay for this food. I prefer it goes to the children. Actually, I'll keep these, they look pretty tasty."

Grumbly Dude huffed and shook Carmella's hand.

"Ms. Sasso, we haven't heard from you since the last superintendent threatened to cancel Halloween. You talking tonight? Press here, too?" he said, scanning the audience.

"I'm here for your droopy eyelids. Calm down, Clarence, you come to me for those," she said, laughing.

"Some discretion, Carmella."

"I'm supporting my niece. She's one of the girls telling you to put period pads in the bathrooms."

Clarence frowned. "Nothing like that on the agenda, but we'd love to hear from you or the girls during public comment. Everyone is welcome to two minutes to say whatever you like then."

Capital UGH. This was bad.

Carmella locked her arm in mine and turned us toward the rows of folding chairs.

"Chiusa una porta si apre un portone," she said and kissed me on the head.

"Yeah, but what if the second door opens to hell, Aunt Carmella? No one ever thinks about what happens next with these sayings. I need to tell our fearless leader." I pointed to Madison.

"Be gentle. She must have come from a funeral. Give her my condolences and lend her your fennel," Carmella said and took a seat in the back row.

I did tell Madison. And it did feel like I had opened a door to hell, because she channeled all her anger through her nostrils and onto my face like an over-coiffed dragon. But as quickly as she'd lost her cool, she then plastered a smile on her face and marched up to Plaid Pants. There was a lot of quiet yelling on Madison's part, nodding from the woman, a finger wagging that would have absolutely landed me and Helen in detention if we could even have pulled it off without laughing. Finally, the woman turned away from Madison and whispered something in the superintendent's ear.

When Madison sat back down, Helen leaned over her shoulder and whispered, "I told you, they don't care."

"They have a very full agenda," Madison hissed back. "It's fine. We're under 'Other Business' now."

There was oodles of Regular Business to do first. I kept myself awake by pretending it was a real Renaissance festival, where the king was doing some serious slaying. Budgets? Chain you up to the stocks. Fall team apparel logo approval? Into the dungeon for a thousand years. Vendor contract bids for paper products and medical supplies? To the tower with you.

The only highlight was Ethan Rogers standing with a bunch of other buzz cuts to get some sportsball award.

"He made a Cuterus Uterus T-shirt, too? Helen, maybe you two are soulmates," I whispered.

"I gave it to him. We sort of ran into each other," Helen said.

"Details!" I said just loud enough so the awards presentation came to a screeching halt and the entire library turned to look at me.

"I want to know everything," I said more quietly, once they started talking about something disgusting called "face-offs" again.

"There was some talk of donut acquisition. I don't know what to make of it," Helen said.

She was playing it cool, but I saw a telltale little upturn on the sides of Helen's mouth. In this town, boys did not make random pastry proposals without a deeper meaning.

"Any board members have other business?" the superintendent asked approximately 1,874 hours later. It was our turn. Or I should say, Madison's turn.

"Stand in a solidarity group behind me," she said.

"Should we line up in the order we're going to speak?" I asked. In the nerdiest act of my entire existence, I'd scribbled a few things down on note cards. They were all in my head anyway, but I find prior use of a gel pen is the best weapon against any in-the-moment brain farts.

Madison said through clenched teeth, "None of you are saying anything after the agenda snafu. Just look like you're listening— Gracie—and you're supportive—Helen."

I crumpled my cards and let them fall from my hand to the indoor-outdoor carpet. Of course I'd pick them up later. But I wanted to say something—do something—and dropping something seemed like the only option.

Madison's presentation was as correct and boring as it had been at the club meeting. The nodding commenced immediately. I felt myself lulled into it like a metronome on a piano. Each board member had their own style. Ms. Laurent of the Plaid Pants jutted out her chin and closed her eyes for a deeper nod at points of emphasis. Grumbly Dude's nod was a side-to-side motion engineered to convey maximum listening. A guy who looked like an older, droopier version of Ethan shifted like he was sitting on eggs. The superintendent tapped his pen and turned to make eye contact with someone on the board whenever Madison got to a point you couldn't argue with.

"How much would this cost?" Grumbly Dude asked.

Madison turned to the "$" tab in her binder. "I've estimated $1,000 a year for the middle school."

Grumbly Dude whistled and leaned back in his chair.

"Fantastic initiative," Ms. Laurent said. "Work with the PTA to fundraise for it. Their executive committee has a breakfast meeting tomorrow. I expect they will be excited to help you with period equity."

The room thundered with nodding.

But then Helen leaned over Madison to speak into the mic.

"We shouldn't have to fundraise for a fundamental right," she said. "A thousand dollars is less than five percent of the middle school football budget you just approved."

"Perfect, we'll fundraise for a pilot program—" Madison hurried to say, but it was too late.

"You're comparing apples to oranges, young lady," the superintendent snapped at Helen.

"More like basic health care to basic brain injuries," Helen said.

The nodding stopped. A tense silence plopped itself into the center of the room.

Then Ethan Rogers's dad laughed. "This is exactly why I ran for school board. To stop people scoring freebies off the backs of taxpayers."

"Do you think toilet paper is a freebie?" Helen called out.

Mr. Rogers's smirk spread. "You will be dealing with this *situation* for a while. Take responsibility for your own bodies, girls."

Ms. Laurent held her hand up. "Let's all take a beat. When Madison first approached me about this issue, I reached out to the school nurse, and good news, we have some pads available in the nurse's offices at the middle and high schools. On days the nurse is not in your building, the principal can get them for you."

"But those pads are only for emergencies, they're literally locked in a cabinet," Helen said, "and they're basically three-inch-thick bandages. Plus you have to get permission to leave class, and teachers won't always let you go, or believe that you have to. Do any of you know how things work at this school?"

Mr. Rogers punched the button on his mic again. "Now we're getting to it. They don't just want products. They want the luxury stuff. When you can't afford to live in this town because our taxes are too high, remember we've turned the middle school bathrooms into spas."

Grumbly Dude squinted. "Excuse me, but what are those things winking on your T-shirts?"

"Uter—" Helen tried to say, but I covered her mouth and yelled myself.

"Cupcakes! Yes, we've reached the pastry portion of our presentation," I said and popped out of our little support group to point out the sweets I'd put in front of each board member. "So, if you could all take a bite and think back to what it was like when you were fighting for change at our age—" but I didn't get further.

Because Madison gasped. Helen cackled. Michael F. gurgled. Isabella dropped her baton on Larisa's head. But mainly it was because of the screaming.

Grumbly Dude was the first to howl. His bite must have been bigger than most, because the raspberry jelly filling spewed out the front of the cupcake and onto the board member sitting diagonally from him. Hers was the second scream. The third was either from the superintendent, who had red jam dribbling down his shirt, or Plaid Pants, who ended up with it on her cheeks somehow. And really, after you get to the third scream in a room full of screaming, the counting isn't useful anymore.

Besides, Madison was pushing us back from the podium, past the snickering sportsball boys and Carmella laughing in the back row over her sandwich, until we were outside at my swag table.

"I can't believe I let you screw this up!" she yelled.

I expected Michael F., Larisa, and Isabella to separate themselves from me and Helen, but everyone stood completely still. Even Helen. And her voice was so cold it made all the little hairs on my arms stand up.

"It was screwed up before we arrived, Madison. Before you even had the idea. They'll put a picture of you standing at the podium in the town paper and congratulate themselves on how involved the students are here. And nothing will ever change."

"We had them talking about a pilot program," Madison said, smoothing her French twist as the five-alarm fire under her cheeks started to go out.

Helen laughed. "You mean where they'll let us beg family and friends for money so we could put pads in the bathrooms for kids to use? Give me a break. If you want to make real change, you need to take bold action."

Madison's eyes narrowed. "We will take what we can get. I will go to that PTA meeting tomorrow."

"So will I," Helen said.

Everyone gasped.

"Helen, I have a dentist appointment," I said, pulling on her shirt.

"I'll speak for both of us," she said without looking back. If she had, she'd see that wasn't what I was asking for.

"You can't come," Madison protested.

"Try to stop me," Helen said.

Then Madison turned to me. "And you. Do you even realize how ridiculous you are? We're trying to do something real, and you make those horrible cupcakes."

"They're conversation starters," I said.

"You think this is funny?" Madison said.

We were a chorus of nos.

"If this change doesn't happen, it is because of you two. Now I need to go back inside for my briefcase," Madison said and stomped away.

The five of us packed up my swag table and karaoke machine in silence. One by one our parentals collected us. Madison didn't speak to anyone as she stormed off to her dad's SUV. Helen and I were the last menstruators standing when Mommy pulled up in the station wagon.

"Ride?" I said.

"I'm gonna walk," Helen said. "Clear my head."

"Good luck tomorrow morning. I'll be there in spirit, but my body will be getting yelled at for not flossing," I said as I climbed into the passenger seat and waved to her.

Mommy gave me a shoulder squeeze. "How did it go?"

"Interestingish."

"Your first brush with politics," she said. "Should we not have been worried? A real snooze?"

"There is a chance Helen started a war with her future father-in-law, and I may have made the board members feel like my cupcakes were having periods on them," I admitted.

Mommy stopped the car short. She turned to me. This was it. Surely this was when she'd share whatever secret knowledge adults have on how everything is supposed to work.

"You know what?" she said, pulling forward again. "I don't even want to know."

But I already knew. Madison and Helen were both right. There was a normal way to make change happen, but it seemed like it wouldn't work for this issue, and Helen's truth-telling and my cupcake catastrophe had sunk that ship to the bottom of the ocean if it ever did have a chance. Maybe we would have to go big like Helen said—1950s cloud-size maxi pad big—to shake things up. Or maybe this PTA deal could be a happy medium to make things better and equal a principal-approved accomplishment even if it wasn't perfect.

# CHAPTER 12

FUNDS

HELEN

The next morning, aka who gets up this early!

After staying up all night thinking about what happened with the school board and getting ready for this next catastrophe, I was trying to catch some sleep while Madison and I waited outside the cafeteria for the PTA meeting. But her sneakers squeaking as she walked back and forth in front of me—one-two-three-four-squeak turn repeat—made it impossible.

"What if they hear you being nervous?" I said without opening my eyes.

That stopped Madison in her tracks. "You should just leave. Also, they can't hear me. Right?"

"Why don't we both leave? If we're begging friends for money, let's just do it."

Madison laughed and patted me on the head. That she kept her hand just shows how tired I really was.

"The parents in there control all fundraising at school. We'll be shut down in a second if we do anything they haven't approved. I heard some scouts tried to sell cookies here when we were still in elementary school and now they're not allowed to have troop meetings on campus."

"Fine, we'll sit tight," I said.

And then we were quiet. Or at least I was.

"If you insist on staying," Madison said, "at least take this seriously. Use your brain for some ideas instead of just tearing mine down. I know you're here to ruin me because your big stink in the gym didn't work out. Do something good, and I promise we can wrestle to the death over a sewage pit or whatever."

It was funny because it wasn't true, even if it was the most logical explanation. I wasn't thinking about our failed stink blub or even Madison. I was here because I cared. Not that I would tell her that, so I was glad when Jasper's mom, Ms. Basset, peeked her head out of the cafeteria doors and gave us a big ol' welcoming wave.

"I have my own ideas," I whispered to Madison as we went in.

"Ones that aren't destructive?" she shot back.

"Join us, girls," Ms. Basset said, taking a seat in a circle of ten lunch chairs, but none open for us. I didn't know how most people could ever be part of this if my parents were any indication. By this time, Mom was already at her office, and Dad was shuffling Seraphine into the car for the drive to school on his way to work.

"We understand the Community Action Club needs to do a little fundraising. What did you have in mind?" she continued.

A few parents smiled at Madison as she opened her binder to the PTA tab.

"As you know," she said, "our project is about period equity. My proposal is to create an online wish list with pads, you share that link with all middle school parents who can purchase them, and the club will stock them in the bathrooms."

It was a direct solution with simplified logistics and no apparent downsides.

They rejected it outright.

"Madison, did you happen to get the wish list idea from when we do the food and litter drive for the animal shelter?" a mom said in a singsong voice I'd be embarrassed to use with a miniature schnauzer.

Madison turned the page in her binder, still smiling. "Must have! Such a great event."

"It is. And we want to avoid any confusion, so . . ." Ms. Basset said, folding her hands primly.

"If there was ever a reason to improve science education in this town, it would be people getting kitty litter and maxi pads confused," I said, but Madison was already on to her next plan.

"Picture it! We turn this cafeteria into a movie theater. Screen a really empowering film. Parents and kids are encouraged to come together. We provide snacks and a post-movie conversation. Everyone donates what they can, and we use that money to buy the pads."

It focused on the school, built community, and had the long-shot potential to actually be fun. They killed it with fire.

"Who is paying for the license to show the film?" Ms. Basset said.

"And the overtime for custodial staff," said another mom.

"And the insurance rider," said another.

"Depending on how many people you're thinking of, we might have to pay for a police officer to direct traffic," Ms. Basset said.

I opened my mouth, but Madison shoved her binder in my face.

"Family pizza night!" Madison said. "We work out a deal with Frank's Pizza where they do a discounted family-style take-out meal exclusively available to Darlington Middle School families. Community Action Club volunteers at the pizzeria to help with the orders, and we get a small cut from each order."

It supported a local business, gave parents a night off from cooking, and had the scientific-guarantee of joy because pizza.

And it literally brought one of the PTA parents to tears.

"Sharon, it's okay, I would never let this happen," Ms. Basset said, consoling her with a pat on her back and a tissue from her purse. "Girls, I'm sure you remember that lunchtime pizza sales fund the fifth-grade class gift to the school, which Sharon is organizing this year. Parents won't want to buy fundraising pizza at night and during the day. I know you don't want this year's fifth graders to fail to maintain the standard of legacy giving that Darlington has come to expect."

The idea that any ten-year-old would care about "legacy giving" unless their parent told them to was the jolt I needed. Part of me was itching to destroy the mathematical basis for their pizza predictions, but they didn't deserve that kind of life-changing clarity.

"I have a great way to avoid whatever is happening right now," I said. "The PTA could just pay for the pads. Madison estimates it will cost a thousand dollars for a year. Give us the money. Cash is good. The end."

"Not an option," Ms. Basset said.

"Sure it is. Last night I broke into my mom's email account—" I said.

The parents gasped.

"Right? A school board meeting plus parent emails, it is amazing I didn't turn to dust. But it gave me the chance to read everything you sent to our parents in the last four years, including all your meeting minutes and budgets. The cost of pads would be less than three percent of last year's fundraising."

"We raise the funds. We decide how they're used," a mom said.

Under normal circumstances, that would get me seeing red, but the thing was, all those emails I read were ridiculous. Because in addition to their pet projects, the PTA bought things like classroom books, water fountains, and gym equipment—the kind of stuff you need to run a school that I assumed the town bought. And these people who can hang out in a school cafeteria at 7:00 a.m. on a weekday ran everything from the school play to assemblies to graduation without getting paid for any of it. It was complicated. I decided against going ballistic and opted to ask them to do their thing already.

"Just decide to use the money on this," I said. "Put it on your Project List and then vote to approve it."

"Project List items must come from a member of the PTA or the school staff," Ms. Basset said.

"You're telling me that as a student, the whole reason this place exists, I have no say in what fundraising happens or what the money is spent on?" I said and turned to Madison, but she was leafing through her binder with great purpose.

I turned back to the parents. "Then one of you put it on the Project List. Or don't you care about period equity?"

"I don't appreciate your tone," Sharon said, sniffing. "I serve on the school's equality and inclusivity committee."

"This isn't about equality. Equality would be me casting a spell to make your son have a period every month, too. Equity means me getting the products I need so I can sit next to him in class when I have mine," I said.

Ms. Basset looked genuinely concerned. "I get it. I donated to a sanitary product drive at our church a few years ago. Some parents will support what you're doing, some parents won't. But official fundraising through the school community is different. Any money you raise takes away from our activities. And if you read all those emails, you know we are asking middle school parents to spend every single week. With families that also have kids at one of the elementary schools or up at the high school, we're also competing with what those PTAs are doing."

Madison cleared her throat. "Just refreshing myself from my notes, Ms. Laurent said, 'I *expect* the PTA will be *excited* to help you with period equity.' Helen, you see that?"

I leaned over her shoulder. She was pointing at the words with her pen. Above it she'd written, *Ask for something they can't say no to NOW.*

"Bake sale! Let us have a bake sale. And be excited about it," I blurted out.

There was a bunch of tittering, chuckling, and even a few guffaws.

"After last night's sticky situation?" Ms. Basset said.

"Last night was a fluke. We'll worry about that," I said. "My point is the PTA stopped holding bake sales three years ago after many months of arguing about store-bought goods."

Now there was murmuring. And Madison's sneakers squeaking in place. And my brain wondering if Ms. Shapiro would notice me taking a nap in the nurse's office all day if I slept under the cot.

Suddenly the cafeteria door popped open. I turned to see the principal peeking her head in.

"Ms. Varone," Ms. Basset called with a big wave, before dropping down to a whisper. "Fine. One bake sale. Friday morning. On the sidewalk."

"Front entrance," Madison said.

"Back entrance," Ms. Basset said.

Madison grabbed my hand and dragged me to the door without thanking them, let alone laying on her usual butt-kissing extravaganza.

Varone stopped us. "Here for Community Action Club?"

"Yes. Truly thankful for the amazing PTA support," Madison said, without a trace of sarcasm.

"It's a dollar store mafia in there," I said. "Are you here to kiss the plastic ring?"

"They like that they can summon me," Ms. Varone said.

"And you like them doing all this work for free," I said.

"Helen, someday you'll learn to be strategic about what you share as the smartest person in the room. But yes, the teachers all get new flip whiteboards this year without me budgeting for it." She took a few steps, then turned back. "Monday morning, let's have an update from you and Gracie. Bring Madison along."

Varone left us, calling out, "Parents! Tell me the latest."

In the hallway Madison opened her binder again. "This could work. We'll just have to sell a lot of sweets. Hey, did you really read all those emails?"

"Want to know how the debate went down for that second gaga dodgeball pit when we were in sixth grade?" I said.

Madison laughed. It sounded real. And maybe that's why I decided to throw her a bone.

"It was cool the way you used what Ms. Laurent said to get them to do the right thing," I said.

"Thank you . . . it is called being prepared. You should try it sometime, 'smartest person in the room.'"

And I took that bone right back. "Too bad it won't work. We'll never sell enough. And now they have an out. They did what we asked and will do no more."

"This is just the beginning—" Madison said.

"When you accept crumbs, don't be surprised when they treat you like a mouse," I said.

Madison groaned. "Oh great, just what we need, a juvenile delinquent Yoda. This will work because we will make it work. But you make sure Gracie doesn't bake anything disgusting. We need these people paying, not puking."

CHAPTER 13

THE MOST AMAZING
BAKING PARTY IN THE UNIVERSE

GRACIE

Thursday night, Pixie Hour

A house full of people.

A kitchen bursting with supplies.

A Sugar Budget decimated by the fifth month of the year.

A menu I designed with the energy of a thousand million suns.

A heart bursting out of my chest, and not just because I had been sneak-munching marzipan all afternoon (against dentist's orders).

"Welcome Community Action Club!" I said to everyone standing around the kitchen island. "My moms have voluntarily banished themselves to moonlight yoga in the back. We have the kitchen to ourselves, with a rather polite request to not burn the house down. Who is ready to bake?"

"I am," Isabella yelled, her baton twirling faster and faster. Luckily, I am a genius host who had thought of everything, including moving the record turntable from the living room to one of the counters. When I turned it on, Isabella's eyes got super big, and she gently placed the baton on it.

"It's twirling," she said and gave me the softest hug.

"And now you have two hands for baking," I said.

"Why does it have to twirl?" Helen asked.

"Why wouldn't it?" Isabella whispered.

"Fair enough," Helen said.

I handed out instructions for each of my creations to Michael F., Larisa, Isabella, and Helen, as well as copies of a message from Madison.

"She can't be here tonight, but she texted me this threat to share with everyone." I held my copy up and then shoved it in my mouth. "So, I wrote it on rice paper with edible ink so you can eat it instead of reading it."

"Gracie, can we talk about this menu, vis-à-vis the school board disaster?" Larisa said, chewing on her rice paper.

"Of course! I'm not stifling anyone's creativity, make what you will, it's just that sometimes I'm so terrified of a blank cookie canvas, having a little direction can help," I said.

And my menu was inspired:

"Cuterus Uterus Cookies: sugar cookies shaped with the uterus cookie cutter that my moms got for my period positivity party, decorated with pink royal icing, red licorice string over the fallopian tubes, and popcorn glued to each ovary with simple syrup. Scrumptious.

"Next we have the Tampretzels: rod pretzels with one half dipped in white chocolate and topped with a marshmallow while the other end is dipped in blue chocolate, which is really just food coloring added to white chocolate. Then you attach a marshmallow rope, and the entire kitchen is a mess."

"You're a menstrual Michelangelo," Helen said.

"Maybe we could make a few simple things, too," Michael F. said. "Like some plain cupcakes with some plain icing?"

I threw my head back and laughed. "Then what will we do with all these mini-menstrual-cups I molded out of marzipan last night?"

"Burn them," Larisa said.

"Ooooooooor make Menstrual Cup-Cakes: funnel-shaped canelés topped with marzipan menstrual cups, but no hidden fillings anywhere, so hopefully no screaming everywhere.

"You could also make Maxi-Grahams: graham crackers dipped in white chocolate, topped with marshmallow fluff, and piped with royal-blue icing for a quilted look. Turns out Mama was totally right about this being better than fondant.

"And last but not least, Adorable Absorbables. These are technically Polish kolaczkis. A lot of people serve them at baby showers because you can make them look like diapers, but with a little food coloring and a whole lot of imagination, they can be period-absorbing undies."

Helen gave me a solo standing ovation. "Show them the sign."

I squealed and pulled the poster board out from behind the fridge.

"The First Annual Darlington Middle School Community Action Club Endo-TREAT-rium Bake Sale Bonanza," I read. "And this summer, we can just swap an *M* for that *TR* and hold a barbeque."

Michael F. made a gurgling noise.

"You okay?" Larisa asked him.

"Just learned some endometrium facts today. I'm good," he said.

"Was it about clots?" Helen said.

"Um, no?" Michael F. looked a little pale.

"Sometimes it doesn't come out as liquid blood, but in chunks," Helen explained.

"Oh . . ." Michael F. said.

"Just be glad Gracie didn't have the supplies for fruit drop cookies," Helen added.

And then everyone was really quiet. It felt like they weren't believing in me, and I got it. Obviously I'd screwed things up. Serving maxi-pad cupcakes to grumbly adults who had atomic bite powers? I hadn't anticipated how big a mistake that would be. I was starting to think that *who* you were making your case to had to factor into *how* you made your case.

The bake sale wouldn't be like the school board meeting. It would be for other kids. Kids like fun! And we needed their support. I knew this was the way to go. I just didn't know if I could mush the words together in a way that would convince anyone other than Helen.

She didn't seem fazed by the silence at all, declaring, "Let's. Get. Baking!"

Isabella raised her hand. "Chocolate-covered pretzels are one of my major food groups, and I just know girls from Cheer will buy them, so genius, Gracie. But I agree with Mike and Larisa. Let's go safe. Plain."

"I hear you," I said. "But it isn't just about the money. We want conversation starters. We need to go glitter. Like for kids to say, *What is this deliciousness?* We'll be all, *That happens to be a medieval Polish pastry reimagined in the shape of a period-absorbing undergarment.* And they're like, *Are you telling me I could replace tampons with something reusable?* And it just goes from there. You wanted to get rid of straws because of the plastic, you should want this to happen."

Isabella nodded at me, but then spoke to Michael F.

"Hey Mike, you sure you're okay?"

He really hadn't been talking this entire time, other than to tell me to be plain.

"A little overwhelmed," he finally squeaked out. "I didn't even know about all these products until tonight. Just trying to listen and understand, since I'm not personally going through it. This is all a little more detailed than we talked about in club, and we don't really talk about this stuff at home. I had to ask my mom where she kept her pads. But it led to this cool if very unsettling discussion between us."

"Why did you ask about her pads?" Helen said.

Michael F. went over to his bag. He opened the front pouch to show where he'd stashed three pads and two tampons.

"At first, she asked if I was putting them in my ears, like, I really don't understand what our parents did for fun when they were younger. But anyway, I told her what we're working on, and that I wanted to keep a few around in case a friend ever needs them. Until we win. Go team."

My heart skipped a beat. Seriously, I didn't think a boy carrying around some quilted plastic could mean that much to me, but there we were. I tried to feed him a marzipan menstrual cup.

"That's okay, Gracie," he said and closed my hand over it, with his hand over mine.

Helen clapped again and we all stood at attention. "Enough about what we're not baking. Gracie said the menu was just for inspo, anyway."

Isabella twirled a pretzel rod. "Team Tampon United!"

"That's what I'm talking about," Helen said. "We will make cool stuff that will get people talking, and also some boring stuff to get their money. Even if this whole thing is ultimately doomed."

And for the rest of the night, we really did have the very best baking party. I am not the least bit ashamed that I stayed next to Michael F. for most of it, or that I could feel the warmth of his hand on mine long after he and everyone else had left for the night.

CHAPTER 14

WELCOME TO THE ENDO-TREAT-RIUM

GRACIE

Friday morning, Coffee Cake Hour

Maybe selling sweets at the back entrance of a school before 8:00 a.m. wasn't the way to outrageous riches, but I knew in my sweet tooth we were about to connect to some hearts about period equity. Now, a food table is a totally different vibe from a swag table. You want to give the feeling of abundance, like someone is about to climb into a confectionery cornucopia by buying a treat in this ecstatic togetherness experience, rather than making it look like an exclusive opportunity. I mean, there is nothing sadder than a picked-over bake sale table. Which is why I brought shoeboxes as risers for the cookie sheets to create a tiered effect and made sure all the pastries were as close together as possible without touching. Even the plain cupcakes looked good.

We were all in our Cuterus Uterus shirts, except for Madison, who looked like a mom who weekends at the mall. Helen set the bubble machine to its disco ball setting while I danced with the Endo-TREAT-rium sign, Isabella handed out my "Which Menstrual Munchie Are You?" flyer, and Larisa and Madison handled the cashbox. Michael F. was missing for a makeup test, but otherwise we were in full force.

WHICH MENSTRUAL MUNCHIE ARE YOU?

* Love convenience and access? Maxi-Graham!
* Do you, for some reason, like
to voluntarily go swimming? Tampretzel!
* Comfy with a side of stretchy? Adorable Absorbables!
* Reuse reuse reuse? Menstrual Cup-Cake!
* All of the above? Cuterus Uterus Cookie!

Remember, these are pastries!
Ask your doc about product options for you!
Community Action Club thanks the PTA
for this chance to build period equity ☺

A few fifth graders walked past us laughing, but one girl circled back, eyeing the Tampretzels. She bought one, took a bite, and immediately proved to have impeccable taste by saying, "This is the perfect combination of salty and sweet *and* crunchy and gooey. Genius."

Her friends all came back and bought some, too. Larisa and Madison gave them the pad project rundown, and then they left. Except that first girl came back a third time.

"I haven't even told my friends yet, but I got it. I'm the first, not in our grade, but our group . . . wait, unless one of them got it but hasn't told me," she said like she was sharing the secrets of the universe.

We were on our way out of middle school, but this girl was the future.

"You think this project is a good idea? Would it help you as a student?" Madison asked her.

The fifth grader nodded solemnly. "Like, Mr. Garland told me I couldn't take my book bag with me to the bathroom last week. I was stuck standing there in the middle of the room with everyone looking at me so I couldn't get the pad out of my bag and then he was all, 'Well?' so I had to just figure it out with wadded-up TP."

"Another way to go is hold your pad up like a trophy and demand tribute to your womb," I said.

The girl laughed and pulled a little satchel out of her bag. "I have this now, but will it be like, *Why are you taking a little ducky bag to the bathroom?* Anyway, I support what you're doing. Both with your eyeliner and the pads."

We high-fived, and I watched her walk into school, feeling triumphant.

"See?" I said, turning back to the other girls at the table. "This really matters. We can get lots of kids interested in change instead of a few of us going to school board meetings. And I knew floating liner wasn't out yet."

Madison rolled her eyes. "It mattered $5. Do your sign dance. Maybe someone will come over thinking you need medical attention."

I did and they came. All the kids who cut across Florence Street had to go past us. Soon we had sold $20 worth of sweets. A bunch of people were quiet when we told them what the project was all about, but a few thought it was awesome and no one said anything nasty. I mean, Titus from my math class shared over a Tampretzel that his mom holds him responsible for her uterus being permanently the size of a four-month-pregnant woman's and brings it up whenever he won't clean his room, but I saw that as more a personal issue than a critique of the pads.

And then there were the Miller twins.

"No one told me there was an idiot convention today. Sign us up," Ruth said, biting into an Adorable Absorbable and dangling a dollar in front of Madison.

"Drop it, Ruth," Madison said, pulling on the cash.

"As you wish," Ruth said and let it go, sending Madison stumbling back.

It wasn't lost on me that more people were coming over to the table now that two popular kids were there.

"We've already made $23, once you pay for that!" I said.

"This place should be mobbed," Ruth said.

"You should have ten times that amount of money," Mary said.

"Not to criticize. Just not how we would do it," Ruth said.

"What would you do?" Helen said.

Mary looked more pensive than I'd ever seen her. "I'm thinking on it, but first a question. I am fully ready for you to devour me for it, but . . . is this really necessary? Enough to put ourselves out there for. Isn't there always a pad around?"

Ruth shook her head and dropped her voice to a whisper. "Straight up, no. I've been thinking about my first time in Pete Jackson's pool since Larisa told me what you all were doing. Not the same as school, but I understand what this is about."

I nearly tackled her. "Tell us everything."

"I thought I was going to die. At first, literally die, and then because I was terrified Pete would tell everyone."

"What happened?" Isabella asked.

"His mother found me crying in the bathroom and told me that if all her kids peeing in the pool didn't kill anyone, a drop of my period blood wouldn't. She gave me a pad and drove me home."

"She is a saint, and mental note to never go in the Jacksons' pee pool," I said.

"Pete never said anything, but a year later, I worry about it every time I see him," Ruth said. "Even if you can afford them, you don't always have them. So I want to get involved, but low-key."

"Okay, here's the deal. Everyone come over for quiz night and next week at lunch we'll help with this disaster," Mary said.

Madison growled. "That would not be an official club activity. You're not even in—"

"Who said you're invited," Mary sneered.

But their argument was interrupted by some moms marching toward the table who didn't look happy. The twins quietly slipped away before they arrived.

"What is this?" one mom said, waving our handout. "My son just asked me what a *menstrual cup* is."

Sounded like the best question ever to me. Gastrodiplomacy for the win! But I kept my celebrating on the inside because these parentals were positively frothing.

"And how is this PTA-approved? I'm on the Curriculum Committee and never heard of it," said another.

"And I'm on the Spring Social Casino Committee."

"We met with the Executive Committee yesterday. Talk to them," Madison said. Even she seemed to lose her chipper adult filter.

"Shut it down. This is disgusting," the first mom said.

"No, see, the fillings are on the outside." I held up a Menstrual Cup-Cake.

"I don't care about your silly sweets. You are exposing my twelve-year-old son to things he isn't ready for," the mom hissed. "What is the point of opting a child out of health class if you're going to corrupt them on the sidewalk?"

"Shut it down," the Casino Mom said, "or we are taking this to Ms. Varone and the board and your parents—"

Larisa laughed. "My parents have more important things to worry about than bake sales and your son talking about truths we have no choice but to live. You have other things to worry about, too."

Team Tampon collectively gasped hard enough we probably created a black hole somewhere in the universe. I thought the moms would explode.

"Like this year's Casino Night," Larisa continued.

The first mom glanced at Casino Mom. "It is our biggest fundraiser of the year."

"More like your biggest crime," Larisa said calmly. "There was a state constitutional amendment on the ballot in November that would have made those kinds of gambling fundraisers legal— and it failed. It was our fall debate topic. That means your casino night is illegal. Should we call your parents?" Larisa said, in what I can only assume is a smartie's version of wrestling smack talk.

The first bell rang as Jasper's mom, Ms. Basset, joined us at the table.

"Janice, we need to talk about this," the first woman said.

"I'll text you all," she said. "Right now, these girls need to get to class."

Madison counted the money. "Forty dollars. At regular store prices we have enough pads for one or two bathrooms for the rest of the school year."

Ms. Basset handed her a small plastic box with BROUGHT TO YOU BY THE DARLINGTON MS PTA written on it in puffy paint.

"Shouldn't this say *By Community Action Club*?" Madison said.

Ms. Basset didn't answer her. "Use this to hold the pads. Very discreet. I think the girls' room in the eighth-grade hallway would be best. Or maybe pick a period-specific bathroom and quietly share that around."

"Instant guarantee no one would ever go in that bathroom," Isabella said.

"Besides, we need all the school bathrooms stocked, every single one," Helen said.

Ms. Basset took two Tampretzels. Without paying. "I can't imagine that ever happening. Remember, something is always better than nothing. And you can bring in your own pads to share with others when you run out. Make sure this is all cleaned up and get to class. And now I get to clean up the parent anger."

The second bell rang. We sent everyone to class with the left-over sweets while Helen and I packed up.

"I knew PTAing wouldn't work, but I'm glad you got to hold a bake sale," she said.

"Why didn't you tell me you didn't think it would work?" I said.

"I've been yelling that since the first club meeting," Helen said. "I hope everyone is ready to superglue themselves to something now."

"But this specifically? You know how much I believe in gastrodiplomacy. Why did we do all this if you didn't believe in it?"

"Well, I didn't want to upset you, and you had a hard time with the cupcakes at the board meeting, so I figured if it is going to fail anyway, at least my bestie had some fun," Helen said.

She smiled at me, but I felt her words right in the place where eating Brie too fast hurts. Here I was, trying to contribute, and it turned out even my best friend might not be taking me seriously. Mama pulled up behind the school. Helen tried to help, but I told her I had it and used my luggage dolly to drag everything to the car. I wasn't sure if I even wanted her to wait for me for the walk to class.

CHAPTER 15

REBIRTH

HELEN

Friday night, aka When Things Get Weird

As the weekend started, it was our turn to kiss the ring. Even if it was a Ring Pop. Madison had accosted me before math to help with applying for charity grants for the pads like we weren't living in a place that could afford this if they cared about our health as much as they cared about sports. I agreed to help with grants if she helped me seal the entire PTA in the superintendent's office with used maxi pads until they gave in to our demands. She screeched and stomped away, so I took that as a maybe.

Either way, I was personally done with the rules. The question was whether to burn them to the ground or step around them. If the Miller twins had any real ideas, we needed to hear them. And that's how Gracie and I found ourselves standing on their front stoop Friday night, clutching our sleeping bags, makeup cases, and some existential quiz night dread.

"I want to be on the record," Gracie said as I rang the bell again, "that when they don't give us time for snacks and ask us bizarro questions, remember that we could have been lying upside down from my old swing set eating spray-can cheese."

The door swung open to reveal Mary and Ruth Miller in

matching hot-pink yoga outfits and dressage-level ponytails, eating matching hot-pink lollipops.

"Finally," Ruth said. "You two look so dumb. I love it."

"Were we supposed to dress like bubble gum sticks, too?" Gracie asked.

"Get in here, turds with a capital U," Mary said, pulling us in by our sleeping bags.

We fudged our way through the family pleasantries on the way in. The twins made it easier than at most houses by repeatedly telling their parents to be quiet and that they were a total embarrassment. That was the thing: As in-your-face demons as they were at home and in the wild, the Miller twins were angels in school. If Madison knew how to work in the system, the Millers had perfected how to keep the system happy enough while still doing whatever they wanted. I hoped that energy could help with the period project, even if there was a 57% chance of us getting an atomic wedgie that night.

Their shared room was bigger than the entire upstairs of my house. It was covered in jewel-tone fabrics, furry throw pillows, and art posters, all centered around a massive craft table. Isabella and Larisa were already there, but no Madison in sight.

I plopped down on a blue faux-fur beanbag chair and yelped at Isabella for almost giving me a lobotomy with her knitting needle.

"It is a crochet hook, actually," she said. "I'm making a super cute shrug. Plus, crochet is good for building finger strength."

"Baton?" Gracie asked her.

"I'm using your turntable idea. My mom was so happy to not have to twirl for me anymore that she got me a portable one,"

Isabella said, pointing to the baton happily rotating at the far end of the twins' room.

Mary handed out clipboards. "Enough small talk. Tonight's quiz is inspired by you all getting a bit jammed up this week: Test Your Wandering Womb IQ."

Gracie tossed the clipboard behind her back. "Or we could skip the quiz and deal with the real stuff happening at school."

Ruth choked on her lollipop. "The deal was we'd help at lunch next week. This is Friday night, and you are trying to bring school into our lives?"

Larisa cleared her throat. "That's my preference as well."

"You're violating the sacred code of sleepovers," Mary said. "Gracie, we even got a cheese plate for you. I mean, we ate it already, but I thought of you at the store."

Gracie swooned onto the beanbag chair beside me.

We all laughed, but I heard a sound behind it. A sound coming from the backyard. I couldn't place what it was exactly. Maybe singing. Or chanting.

"Did you hear that?" Isabella asked.

Ruth nodded and grabbed her hand. "Can your hook be a weapon?"

"If you saw the sweaters my mom made, you would definitely say yes," Isabella said.

We got up from the table and huddled together, drawing closer and closer to one another as we made our way to the window. The backyard was complete darkness. My chest tightened as Mary lifted the bottom window pane a few inches.

"Donuts! Donuts! Donuts!"

I peeked over Mary's shoulder and saw a group of boys on the grass below.

"Finally!" one of them called up, spotting us. "We've been out here for like five minutes!"

"Five minutes too long," Mary said.

"Go home, goobers," Ruth yelled. She grabbed a jar of glitter and was about to rain it down on them when Mary stopped her.

"They're not worth the eco-friendly stuff," Mary said.

"Come on!" yelled another boy. "We won our game. Let's go get donuts!"

"Who is that?" Larisa asked.

Ruth turned to us all. "There's Jasper, Lucas, Ethan . . ."

I grabbed Gracie's hand and she squeezed mine back.

". . . and two also-rans," Ruth continued.

Mary leaned out the window. "No one is interested in your janky donuts. We're having an amazing party with girls who glow."

"Good. Make sure there is a girl for each of us to hang out with." This time I recognized Jasper's voice saying that gross nonsense. The rest of them whooped like it was the funniest thing they'd ever heard.

I pressed my face to the glass, hopeful that Ethan was telling the other boys to cut it out. Instead, he was whooping with the rest of them. But maybe he didn't mean it. Maybe he was just showing off the way these boys all try to out-dumb each other.

"Dude! Ethan! Helen is there," a boy said. "Probably planning her period revolution."

"Gross, man. Stop," Ethan said.

"This is ridiculous! Ruth, Cruller Castle now!" Jasper said.

"I get not wasting high-quality glitter, but I'm fine parting with my iced tea," Larisa said.

"Larisa!" we squealed in delighted shock. But there was no time to lose. We each grabbed whatever drinks we had and rained justice upon those fools. Iced tea, water, soda. Those chumps got it all and ran for cover. I saw Ethan take off his jacket and turn it inside out as he followed.

Now we were the ones laughing and hollering. It felt like a weight had been lifted from my chest. We sat back down at the table.

"Mary, do not hand me another clipboard," Larisa said. Her voice had such weight even those motormouths didn't respond. No wonder she ran the Debate Club.

"You okay?" Gracie asked me softly, but everyone heard.

"What's the damage?" Isabella asked.

Ruth grabbed my chin. "No. You have crush eyes. For that dufus?"

"My fantasy hasn't reached naming our children yet, but definitely getting matching PhD levels of crush," I said.

"A PhD in what? Almost tying his shoes?" Mary said.

"I like his style," I said.

"The jacket is fake," Mary said.

"Or he murdered an animal for it," Ruth said.

"But he wore the Cuterus Uterus shirt at the school board meeting. He can say the word *period* out loud easier than I can. That has to mean something, right?" I asked, and I truly meant it as a question, because I didn't know anymore.

"Now we're into dudes just because they can say the word *period* when we have to live it? Am I the only one who is so over this?" Larisa said. "I might not be into the whole girl chat thing, in fact I expect to break out into hives shortly, but I really care about equity issues. Our current strategy on the pads won't work."

Ruth shook her head. "I care, too, but last week you asked me to go to the school board meeting to talk about one of the most private things in existence and at that bake sale you might as well have held signs saying, *Uptight moms, come yell at me.*"

"What if it being private is the problem? We talk about periods as if it is this thing in a little glass box, but it is really just us existing," Isabella said. "So maybe we need to get personal."

I hadn't thought about it that way. Maybe my voice could make it easier for other people to use their own voices by breaking that glass box around the word *period*.

But I kept coming back to the feeling that I shouldn't have to talk about it. That I shouldn't have to tell my teacher why I have to go to the bathroom, that I shouldn't have had to tell Varone why I was in the hallway, that I shouldn't have to tell the nurse what's going on to get a pad, and that I really really really should not have to stand up in front of our entire town and share my personal bathroom experiences in a recorded meeting posted for all the world to see—all just to get access to sanitary supplies that they already know we need.

"But only if that's what people are cool with sharing," I finally said. "I don't think anyone is entitled to the tale of my bloody pants. I shouldn't have to perform to make them feel so I get my basic needs at school met. And someone shouldn't have to announce which bathroom they use to make sure pads are in there."

"And, like, I would be cool dressing in a full-body uterus costume and spraying everyone with red Silly String to make the point," Gracie said and gave me a fist bump.

"And not everyone can afford the products they need, but do I need to give the world a rundown of our family finances?" Larisa said. "No offense, but we don't all have bedrooms like this. I share a normal-size one with my two sisters so we can go to school here. At my old school, I got all kinds of stuff from my teacher's supply cart, like pads and deodorant and toothbrushes, which really helped, but then I found out she was paying for it all herself and I felt guilty. I'm so sick of feeling not enough and guilty at the same time."

Larisa always seemed so guarded that it got me in all my feelings, limited as they were, to hear her talk like this. If we didn't talk about periods at school, we definitely didn't talk about who had enough and who went without. Gracie was the only person who knew there were fights about money at my home, but I didn't even share with her the way Larisa was opening her heart to all of us.

Larisa continued. "Here, I've had to get a stack of pads from Ms. Shapiro. I don't know what other girls do if they need pads and she doesn't have more. I don't want to rely on her stash, but being smart doesn't mean you have any money in this town."

"Can I get that on a T-shirt, please?" I said. "Preferably one I don't have to pay for."

"We shouldn't even have to think about where to get a pad. There is a cost we pay for that worry and planning. Boys don't even get the bill," Larisa said.

"Whoa," Ruth said, framing her hands around Larisa's head. "I like your brain. And I'm in. We need something creative that brings lots more people in. You had, what, like a handful of people at the school board meeting? Twentyish at the bake sale? There are a thousand kids at our school. I'm guessing a lot more need to ask for something to make it happen."

"And no PowerPoints or anything else that could remotely count as school," Mary added. "And nothing tee-hee and giggles. We're asking people with periods to say something they might get a hard time for. Be fun, but, like, treat people seriously."

Isabella had picked up her crocheting again. And as I watched her hands whirl through the yarn, it came to me. Something big. Something that went directly to how everyone took care of themselves in the bathroom. Something that could not be ignored.

"Do you have more of those hooks and balls of yarn, like for a bunch of kids?" I asked.

Isabella squealed. "I have a major stash from my Grams. Ahhhh! I have so been wanting to start a crochet circle, but no one ever seemed into it."

I grabbed a pencil and paper and sketched out a quick pattern. I didn't know the names of the stitches, but I could draw them. Isabella definitely got where I was going, because she dropped her hook and said, "Oh no."

"Oh yes. We won't glue those bathrooms shut until the school puts maxi pads in them. We will crochet an army of uteruses to do the work for us, replacing toilet paper rolls at school with our craftivist art. Let me know how this feels in your brains: Operation Crocheterus."

"It feels like a dinosaur who wears cat-eye glasses and reads romance novels just lit the place on fire," Gracie said.

"It feels like a level-nine plan. Let's start back at a five," Mary said.

"Remember? We said fun?" Ruth said.

This sounded like the height of fun to me, but I decided to dig deeper. Less prankful, more purposeful.

"What if we build on what's already in the school—those massive pads in the nurse's cabinet," I offered.

"Perfect," Isabella said. "If we show how those pads, and the ones we fundraised for, are used, that will be evidence that students need pads in all the bathrooms. A win-win for everyone."

"Here's how it will go," I cut in. "Mary and Ruth get the key to the nurse's supply cabinet from the office the next time you're working as aides. Gracie and I fake double food poisoning to get sent to the nurse. While Ms. Shapiro is treating us, Isabella and Larisa sneak into the nurse's office, use the key on the cabinet, and liberate the maxi pads. Gracie and I miraculously recover, and then the four of us put the pads in all the bathrooms while Mary and Ruth replace the key in the office before anyone misses it. Is Monday good for everyone?"

Isabella put her arm around my shoulder and squeezed. "Still a little too big."

"Also, not the point," Ruth said. "Whatever we're doing has to get other kids into it, so it needs to be public, not sneaky."

"Excitement is way more important than getting the elephant pads into the wild," Mary agreed. "What can we do where kids already are that would get back to the school board so they'd need to deal with it? I was thinking about holding a mini-march, but we would get stopped in the hallway before we even got started."

"Plus, we would have to get people to show up," Ruth said.

"Let's flip it," Gracie said. "I love doing that when there's a problem I can't figure out."

She pulled on an imaginary blazer, balanced imaginary oversize glasses on her nose, and teased her hair with her hands.

"Girls, we're doing something innovative here," Gracie said in her best Ms. Varone voice. "If I wanted to make you listen, I'd do it in a place you couldn't leave."

"An assembly!" Isabella said.

"OMG, yes. Only we can't call one of those as students," Ruth said.

Gracie hitched up her invisible pantyhose. "No problem, there are plenty of places you're trapped to listen."

"The PA system, like for morning announcements during homeroom. Everyone would hear," Larisa said.

"Not to keep being a downer, but we'd never get to the mic in the first place," Mary said.

"Where else are kids trapped but have the freedom to talk?" Gracie said.

We all looked at each other and said it at the same time: "Lunch!"

Mary crossed her arms. "That's it. We already rule the caf."

"Will you lead it?" Larisa asked Mary and Ruth.

I could feel the telepathy working between them as the twins locked eyes. They weren't saying yes. People wanted to follow them, but you didn't think of those girls being out in front, putting their names on things the way Madison did.

"I will!"

The voice didn't come from either of the Millers.

It was Gracie!

"Amazing!" Isabella said and everyone agreed as she continued, "I really like how the pads were the start, but not the end, when you explained things."

I wanted to argue, to protect Gracie. Isabella didn't even have lunch with us, so I don't know why she would put Gracie out there like that. But what was the alternative? I was still firmly a no on talking about my period in front of everyone. But for my bestie, would I?

Before I could come up with a good counterpoint, though, Gracie beat me to it again.

"Thank you all for believing in me!" she cheered.

CHAPTER 16

FULFILLMENT

HELEN

Monday morning, aka at least I wasn't in science

It was time for our punishment meeting with the principal. Madison was already sitting at the talking table when Gracie and I arrived. At the sleepover, we'd all agreed, even Larisa, to sidestep Madison for our next action. But we couldn't avoid her everywhere.

"What if I spill the beans," Gracie said through a super-fake smile.

"I'll do the talking," I whispered as we took our seats.

The sad plastic PTA box for the pads sat in the middle of the table.

"We're past the two-week mark, and here is a physical manifestation of your accomplishment," Ms. Varone said, gesturing to the puffy-painted disappointment. I expected her to laugh, but she was beaming at us. "Also, I have not had a single staff member complain to me about either of you in days. Tell me all about it."

Madison opened her mouth, but the principal shook her head.

"I want to hear from them first."

I cleared my throat and dove in. "We attended a club meeting, contributed ideas, supported Madison at the board meeting,

convinced the PTA to let us fundraise, and held a delightfully disgusting bake sale to buy these pads." It sounded like we had been
very busy.

Madison had been waggling her foot the entire time Varone
and I talked and busted out now. I braced myself for the impact
of her accusing us of screwing everything up.

But she said, "This is just the beginning. Next, we'll show how
all bathrooms should have pads provided by the school district."

"Excellent, and you didn't do it by having your parents open
their checkbooks," Ms. Varone said, pointing at me and Gracie.
Given that my parents had spent the night before arguing about
car payments until Seraphine came out of her room crying, Ms.
Varone had nothing to worry about.

"I don't have baking funds for the rest of the year, but it was a
tasty way to go," Gracie said.

"Do you have any suggestions for how we can complete the
project?" Madison said.

A brilliant strategy. Get the adults talking when what they
really want is information from you.

"Not covering board members in red jam again is a good
option. Or making parents email me that their sons shouldn't
know about menstrual cups. Girls, you're asking to be trusted
with knowing what is best for the school, the budget, and your-
selves, but then behaving in some ways like you shouldn't be
trusted with anything. Is the larger issue starting to come into
focus?" Ms. Varone said.

"Vaguely, like it is just around the corner, but I don't like it so
I keep walking," Gracie said.

Ms. Varone shook her head. "Try this. You've got to get the community to believe the board would be foolish to not do what you're advocating for. It needs to be the obvious choice, and better yet, make it sound like something they're already planning. At least, that's what I'm doing in my contract negotiations."

Those two things couldn't be more different. She was an adult, literally running the entire place, the people in charge of the school district cared about her, and if they wanted her to be principal, they would give her what she asked for. We didn't have someone with power asking for the pads.

"Will you stand up at the next board meeting with us and ask for this change?" I said.

Ms. Varone sat back in her chair and crossed her arms. "I could, but I won't."

"Because you don't want us cutting into your profits like the PTA," I said.

"No, Helen, I'm not a dollar store administrator. The board can find a way to pay for this, and I can weather the irate parent emails for something worthwhile. There is a difference, though, between thinking something is good and putting yourself out there publicly for it. Think about when you ask your parents for something. If you ask for everything all day long, you become part of the background noise and it is easy for them to tune you out. One of my jobs is asking for the most important things I can get," Ms. Varone said.

"This isn't important to you?" Gracie asked. She sounded a little crushed. It would continue to happen as long as she expected anything more than nothing from these chumps running our lives.

"I'm responsible for the entire school. For example, today I meet with school board members to prove the HVAC is kaput. Ah, we have state air quality standards to meet, so they must pay. Is it more important than something like adding another middle school sports team? Definitely, but there will be tons of parents screaming at the board in support if I ask for that."

"What if we were using our own money on monthly bake sales so we could buy toilet paper? Wouldn't that sound ridiculous?" I said.

Ms. Varone pushed the puffy-paint box toward me and stood up from the table.

"But that isn't what's happening, Helen. In any event, punishment complete. I was hoping it would take you longer, but you did it," she said.

Madison grabbed the box. "*They're* getting credit for this?"

"No pads before Helen and Gracie got involved, now there are pads. Accomplishment."

The girl turned so red so fast I thought she might explode. What I didn't know was why she even cared. Me and Gracie being involved didn't take anything away from her. But before I'd even finished my thought, Madison thanked Ms. Varone and promised to keep her up-to-date. Gracie followed her out, but the principal held her hand up for me to stay, closing the door behind them.

"Sage Academy for Girls has been in touch. Impressive place."

That was not at all what I'd been expecting her to say. I'd spent so much time listening to Gracie practice her speech and helping her make flyers over the weekend that I had barely thought of my parent problems. But here they were, using the principal as a weapon. I'm sure that place was fine, but it wouldn't be with Gracie, which was the only place I wanted to be, and I would never hear the end of it if my parents shelled out that kind of cash and I didn't discover a new planet or write a bestseller or not get into trouble.

"The pamphlet says it's built out of millions of bricks," I said.

"I sent your transcripts over as requested. Now they've asked for your full file," Ms. Varone said.

Okay. Things were moving much more quickly than Mom had let on. I knew she'd called the school again after Seraphine ratted on me for the completely hypothetical but admittedly priced-out plan of going all biblical on the library with red paint, but I didn't realize we were in the vetting stage.

There would be a path out. I needed a minute to find myself in the maze first.

"This would be a fresh start for you," Ms. Varone said. "Sage Academy has much better academics than our high school, but you didn't hear that from me. I think you'll excel there."

"I'll also start calling myself 'Muffy' and convert to an entirely plaid lifestyle."

"How about meeting the girls before you judge them?" Ms. Varone said, opening the door.

"Make sure you include the most colorful portions of my file for them. Use neon tabs. Make the misdemeanors pop," I said, backing into the hallway where Gracie waited.

"Are you okay?" Gracie asked. "I figured it must be bad if she wanted to talk to you alone."

"It was nothing," I said, giving the best friend I could ever ask for the world's biggest hug, but she kept staring out the window toward the parking lot.

"You returning to Earth anytime soon, or should I join you on Zebulon 9?" I asked.

"Varone was so chill. She even seemed happy. Like she's done with us for the year. So, the noodles in my brain are twirling into a thought," Gracie said.

"Leave it?"

"Right?"

I realized that's what had been bothering me in the meeting. Maybe Varone cared more about not having to deal with us than with our actual "accomplishments." But wouldn't nonstop detention have done that?

"At the beginning," I said, "I was totally there on leaving it, remember? But now I care. You and my unruly uterus got me to care when I couldn't see it myself. And Varone made it clear she's not doing anything more and she even thinks it is a good idea."

"This project matters to me, a lot, but us together matters the most," Gracie said.

Sage Academy would be way worse than closing my eyes and drooling my way through the next month, but I just didn't believe my parents could make good on the threat. If you can't make a car payment, you can't pay for private school. I didn't want to worry Gracie, though. Plus, she needed this. She was so excited getting her speech ready all weekend. I hooked my arm in hers and turned us toward homeroom.

"Obviously, but it is just sitting on the tables and talking to people at lunch about period equity, not committing a crime," I said.

That finally got a Gracie smile. "We're already loud and stupid in the cafeteria on the daily."

"Exactly, so how much trouble can we get into for being loud and smart for a change?"

CHAPTER 17

SIT-IN & SHOUT OUT

GRACIE

Monday lunch, Cheese Hour

I had never been so excited for lunch, and I basically live for lunch. It was like Taco Tuesday invited Pizza Friday over for a dance party with Grilled Cheese Bar deejaying. Because Helen was right. How much additional trouble could a lunch sit-in cause when we regularly got yelled at for excessive laughing and the boys could say whatever vulgar nonsense wormed through their brains without consequence?

I got myself a heaping plate of never-ending spaghetti with extra meatballs and found Helen talking to the Millers at their table in the middle of the cafeteria.

"It is so loud over here," Helen said.

"Yeah, but we can see and hear everything going on. Not everyone has the luxury of being social nomads like you two," Mary said.

She and Ruth took off their sweaters to reveal dazzling Cuterus Uterus shirts. They'd copied Helen's adorable design using a bajillion sequins. They had a bag full of them.

"Mom was furious," Ruth said. "She was all, 'Why are you raiding my closet for red shirts,' and I said, 'Why don't you love me enough to know red is my favorite color, do you even realize you have two daughters with two personalities,' and then she helped us find some more."

Mary high-fived her. "It was an expert deployment of twin guilt. Now expect Mom to buy you red junk for every holiday ever."

People came over to get shirts, chat with the twins, and head back to their own tables. There were Girl Scout lifers, gamers from Pixels & Pikachus, and everyone in between, including boys. Not all kids you'd expect to get involved in something like that.

"We've been working the group texts all weekend," Mary told us between visits, "but we kept it off social. Twenty kids in our lunch section are in for wearing a cute top and sitting in solidarity. Don't blow it."

"I'm sharing factoids and getting a little personal on why this issue matters," I said, giving everyone stacks of the new glitterati handout I'd made from my own research on how it would cost kids who menstruate thousands more dollars over our lives to pay for pads, tampons, and ruined undies.

> ### THE BLOODY TRUTH ABOUT
> ### MONEY & MENSTRUATION
>
> - People who menstruate have to spend 1,000s of dollars on period products—look at the people who don't menstruate around you.
> What will they get to spend that money on?
> - Kids who can't afford products use the ones they have longer than the boxes say to, and sometimes use stuff like rags and

paper towels. NO SURPRISE they can get infections
that cost even more!

• Missing school because of periods hurts our education*—yet adults
keep telling us our educations determine how much money we make.
So why don't they give us what we need to go to class?
*You have no idea how hard it was for me to write that, but when
truth is coursing through your fingers, you just promise yourself
you'll cut an extra class to make up for it.

That was the cost if nothing went wrong. I'd seen Mama have to take a sick day or drag herself to the office and even court with one of those self-stick heating pads on her belly. Since my body felt like a deck full of wild cards to begin with, I might pay thousands more for things like medical care to deal with bad cramps and missing work for painful periods. I was half terrified everyone was believing in me to lead this thing, and half thrilled by these facts I found with my own eyeballs. Pads were honestly the least the school could do for students.

Larisa walked up to the table then, looking more intense than usual as she sat down. "Ran into Madison. She knows. She knows we didn't tell her, and she's not happy. Maybe we should have included her?"

Mary laughed. "She knows we don't follow her so she wouldn't be involved. Madison needs to accept that this project is way beyond her now."

"Or she doesn't have to accept it. Who cares. We got you the supporters, let's do this," Ruth said.

Helen did one of those wicked whistles with her fingers in her mouth that should get her out of having to take music.

Right on cue, everyone wearing a Cuterus Uterus shirt got up and sat on top of their lunch tables, just like the Millers had asked. There was a bunch of giggling and then gradually a silence fell over the room. It was so eerie that I forgot they were waiting for me. Finally, I jumped onto my chair.

"Hey, my name is Gracie," I called out. "I'm an eighth grader, and I'm asking for—check that—I'm *demanding* period equity. Anyone who has a period should get whatever they need to take care of their period at school. No cost. No hassle. Maxi pads in every bathroom, for starters!"

Then I got even louder. "Who needs to buy pads every month?"

"Me!" yelled Mary, Ruth, Helen, Larisa, and a bunch of the girls in T-shirts. I looked out at a sea of faces, some confused, embarrassed, annoyed—but a lot of them were paying attention.

"Does it matter whether you can afford them?" I yelled.

"No!"

"Who has started your period only to realize you didn't have a pad?"

"Me!" came the callback in chorus, but it wasn't only the girls in T-shirts now. Small pockets of people were yelling back from all over the lunchroom.

"Were there pads in the bathroom?"

"No!"

"Who has felt scared, ashamed, and alone on your period?"

"Me!"

"Me too!" I hollered. "And this is just the start of what period equity means to me. I'm a full-on human whose body doesn't care if it's the first or last ten minutes of class. I need to go to the bathroom when I need to go. I'm doubled over for two days a month with cramps. Imagine if I was like that for some other reason. Wouldn't we expect the school to make sure I was getting what I needed to be a fully engaged student? Can we all imagine what it would really take for kids who have periods to be in the same place as kids who don't?

"But let's start here. I demand that the maxi pads locked in the nurse's office be liberated and put where we'll actually use them."

It felt like the sun was bursting through my heart. It also felt like someone was pulling on my pant leg. In fact, it was Coach Kline.

"Down. Now," he said through a wad of gum.

"I'm in the middle of a sit-in, Coach."

"The only sit-in that matters is your butt in this chair," he said and then spoke to the room. "Womanhood. Empowerment. The other E-word you said. Equity, right. But no sneakers on the chairs, folks, and no butts on the tables. This is an eating room."

I didn't get down. Helen jumped onto the chair next to mine. "We stand for justice. Release-the-Pads! Release-the-Pads!"

She yelled it again and again. Other kids stood on their chairs and joined in. Coach Kline shook his head and unlatched his walkie-talkie from his belt.

I didn't hear what he said, because at that point there were more than fifty kids chanting, "Release-the-Pads!" My chest rose and fell with their words, my own voice ringing out with hope. The school board couldn't ignore that many voices. I pumped my fist in the air and was promptly hit right between the eyes with something. I held out my hand as it rolled down my nose. A spitball landed in my palm. I looked across the room. Jasper and some other boys were laughing like hyenas.

Standing next to me, Coach Kline was next.

"That's detention for you, Mr. Basset," he said, rubbing his neck where there had been a direct hit.

I looked around the room and saw straws unsheathed from cups, milk containers, and even the dreaded juice boxes. Kids paired up to create ammunition from wrappers and napkins and launch the attacks. The air around us filled with spittle-soaked paper bits. I grabbed Helen's hand, dropped to the floor, and rolled under our table where the rest of Team Tampon had taken cover.

"How do we stop this?" Larisa asked.

"Why would we want to?" Helen said.

I didn't know what was going through that beautiful brain of hers. Had it started automatically bending toward chaos, the way a flower turns to the sun? And then, right in front of my face, an eensie ice chip hit the floor. And then another.

"Now, this would have been a prankuation to remember," Helen said as a half-eaten hero landed in front of her. Did that mean the paper and ice projectiles had run out?

And just like that, our peaceful protest that had turned into a spitball assault ratcheted up to a full-fledged food fight. On the worst possible day. Never-ending pasta meant never-ending food to launch. Spaghetti shot through the air like water from a fountain. Red sauce and alfredo splattered tabletops until they looked like melted candy canes oozing onto the floor.

It hit me that Helen was right. A month ago, this would have been a dream come true. A student earnestly pouring their heart out, trying to lead others in changing the school, brought down by mayhem? I would have cheered. Crashing an entire lunchroom in absolute chaos, using spitballs to finish our Darlington prank career—the very thing that had brought Helen and me together in the first place—well, it would have been the closest I'd ever get to becoming a poet.

But now I was that earnest student. And this was a cause I cared about. And I was falling into an existential crisis even though I was already on the floor when the loudest, most ear-piercing, terror-inducing whistle ever produced by human lips brought all the noise to a halt. The kind of whistle Helen would surely produce one day, if she kept practicing. Crawling out from under the table, I saw Ms. Varone standing in the lunchroom doorway with three members of the school board. We locked eyes.

"Enough!" she barked. The room was dead silent for five seconds—until a pile of penne smacked her right on the cheek.

The next ten minutes flew by. Ms. Varone had teachers deploy industrial-size paper towel rolls to the four corners of the room and ordered everyone to clean their own space and themselves. The head custodian, Mr. Allen, came in with two rolling carts full of buckets and we wiped down the walls and floor. Not a single kid said a word.

When the bell rang, Ms. Varone stopped Helen and me at the door.

"Oh, you two, you're the girls who came begging for a handout, and now look what you're costing us," Mr. Rogers, Ethan's dad and one of the school board members, said. "Is this how you run our middle school, Ms. Varone, letting these little hellions destroy the place?"

"We didn't do it," Helen said. "Forget about starting it. We didn't have any straws to spitball and had taken cover before any food flew. It was a bunch of jocks. Maybe your son was there."

That was the moment I learned Ms. Varone surely had children of her own. She gave Helen the Look. The one that burrows into your soul and whispers, *You're in store for punishments not even invented yet if you don't shut it.*

"Members of the school board, I apologize for this disruption. Please make your way over to the HVAC compressors. The engineer is waiting for us. I'll join you shortly, and I assure you we will get to the bottom of this," Ms. Varone said.

"I expect you to deal with these two. Severely," Mr. Rogers said on his way out.

"Girls," Ms. Varone said in a quiet voice when we were alone. "It seems our little experiment failed."

"I don't know, a lot of kids were really into the issue before the first spitball flew," I said.

"You misunderstand. The punishment portion of the experiment didn't work. Mere hours after I acknowledged your accomplishment, you've caused this catastrophe. Let's try this. I'm separating you two for the rest of the year."

"What if we do more fundraising? I'll hold bake sales forever to pay for pads," Helen said.

"Do you honestly believe the school board will approve

anything related to what you've done?" Ms. Varone said. "I just hope you're not worse apart than together."

"Detention every day until the end of the year," Helen countered.

Ms. Varone didn't respond to her. She must have made up her mind about who was at fault the minute she saw us in the room.

She turned to me. "Gracie."

I couldn't look up. If I did, tears would start pouring out and never stop.

"I'll email your parents a new schedule, because Helen—"

When your world is crushed into oblivion, do the specifics really matter? But I finished the principal's thought for her anyway.

"Helen is in the smart classes. You can put me anywhere. I get it."

CHAPTER 18

SPLIT

HELEN

*Monday afternoon, aka when everything went
sideways and inside out and bad bad bad*

"The important thing is to not freak out," I said at the Cruller
Castle a few hours later.

After school, Gracie and I skipped the bus, taking the long way
back to her house. We had exactly $1.25 between us for two mini-
glazed donuts, and there was a table free in the Turret. I started to
calm down as soon as the first bite hit my belly.

"Quick programming update," Gracie said. "I've been screaming 'Ahhhhhhhhhhhhhhhhhhhhhhh' in my brain, on a loop,
since the first spitball flew."

Her big baby browns were bloodshot. Dark circles had appeared
under them since the cafeteria disaster. Gracie had never looked so
drained in all the years we'd been friends.

"Varone already gave us an out," I said. "She's worried we'll be
worse on our own. We can easily show her she's right."

Gracie looked up, like there might be answers falling gently
toward us from the ceiling.

"We would have to do more bad stuff to show her she's right, but in this case, it would be even worse because we're doing the bad stuff specifically to be bad, not for fun. Is this what philosophers do? Because my temples are killing me."

I ran through all our conversations with the principal, trying to find another out.

"She wanted to be innovative. Splitting up kids who get in trouble together isn't breaking any ground. You and I will invent a better punishment."

"Helen, I honestly don't think I can design my own torture chamber. What else is your beautiful brain conjuring?"

"There was something about restorative justice. What if we volunteered to cook in the cafeteria to make up for the wasted food?"

"Do you think Ms. Costello is over the grease fire I started in sixth grade?" Gracie said.

I was beginning to get Varone's point. Our options to get out of trouble now were somewhat limited by all the prior trouble we had caused. The only other option was our parents. But not my parents, unless I had been adopted by some much more understanding family since breakfast.

"What will your moms say?" I asked.

Gracie squeezed her whole face with her little doll hands. "My guess is I'm in for a 'we're disappointed' lecture."

"Can't they retire those already?"

"They know we're capable of so much more," Gracie said. She gave me the first smile I'd seen all afternoon.

"By the way, you were awesome during the sit-in. Everyone was listening to what you had to say."

"I was awesome," she agreed, then sat up a little straighter. "What effect will these class changes have on me? Surely the parentals will care about that."

"Now you're baking with salted butter."

"You know, there is the minor point that we didn't actually do what we're being punished for. That food fight had nothing to do with our sit-in."

"You want to go for it? Think your moms will help us talk Varone out of her terrible divide-and-conquer scheme?" I said.

"Will you back me up?" Gracie said.

"I will always be there for you. Also, I really do not want to go home right now," I said.

By the time we reached Gracie's house, we were ready to go. She had a butterflied plan—because "bulleted" sounded very aggressive—of how she'd make the case.

"Mommy! You will not believe what happened," she said as we twirled through the front door.

But it looked like they would definitely believe it. Her parents were sitting at their kitchen island, the phone perched between them, mugs of tea in their hands. Not the handles in their hands, but the round part. Concerned grip.

"Mama, you are home so early," Gracie said, giving her a hug.

"I came home when Mommy called me. After she talked to your principal."

"Good. Then you know the situation," Gracie started. But her mom cut her off and turned to me.

"You should head home, Helen," Mama said.

"Am I wearing my invisibility cloak?" Gracie said, patting her arms. "I'm right here, and I want Helen right here."

Her mom wrapped her arm around Gracie. "Our family needs to talk," Mommy said.

Gracie pushed back. "We have important things to tell you. Like first of all, neither of us did any spitballs—"

"Like all the other times you got in trouble for spitballs?" Mama said.

Gracie sputtered, "Or threw any food. And you're always telling me to express myself, and today I used my voice for good."

"You were using it for chaos, as usual," Mama yelled.

"No," Gracie said. "It was the kind of peaceful protest you told me you did back when you met." Her voice broke on the last word. Tears were welling in her eyes. I kept expecting them to form in mine as well, but all I felt was a dark emptiness crawling through me.

"It was another bad choice," Mama said, sounding as sad as Gracie did.

"I'm not choosing to be apart from Helen. Do you not understand what she means to me? You know, Mommy, how it feels to be separated from Aunt Carmella. It hurts your heart."

"That's different. We're adults, and she is my sister," Mommy said.

"Then this is worse. You always used to ask me questions about being an only child, but the truth is I don't even think about it. Helen is whatever is closer than a sister to me. And, and my last butterfly is that all these changes to my schedule will really impact—" Gracie tried to continue.

But Mama shook her head. "I called Ms. Varone back and told

160

her to make whatever changes are necessary. You'll figure out how to live with them."

"Did you even stand up for me?" Gracie said.

"Enough is enough," Mama said. "I'm going for a drive."

Gracie covered her mouth with both hands. Mommy tried to hold her, but Gracie sank to the floor. I wanted to grab her and hold her so she would hold me back, so if it had to feel like we were floating in space with no idea of which way led to an escape hatch, at least we'd be floating together. But I wasn't welcome in that moment, in that house. Not that I was welcome at my home, either. But that's where my stuff was, so that's where I went.

My plan was to keep my head down and take the shouting without saying a word in response. If Gracie's parents didn't care that we didn't do it, there was no way mine would.

I ran through the route to my room in my head. The click of the front door from my key would lead to the squeak of my mom's kitchen chair as she pushed back. She'd reach the foyer as I kicked my second shoe off, but not before my backpack hit the rack. Head down, I could make it to the fridge for whatever was edible without a utensil. No drink, because then I'd have to go to the bathroom. Front door to my bed was doable in less than a minute if I focused. I stopped in front of Michael F.'s house and tilted my head back, so that any tears forming might drain into my eye sockets. When I looked back down, I noticed my window was open. The Tiny Terror herself was sitting on the sill.

"I figured you would want to come in this way," Seraphine said in a sweet voice I hadn't heard in forever. Even in the twilight I could see she'd been crying.

"How bad is it in there?" I asked.

"I would say the worst," Seraphine said.

I climbed in and hunched over, so I could sit on the sill facing her. She handed me Mr. Wigglesworth. His soft fur was crisscrossed by tire tracks and when I buried my face in his glowworm nose like I had thousands of times before, he smelled less like my tears and more like motor oil.

"Who did he lose a fight to?" I said.

"I stuck him on the front of my bike, which I renamed the Pirate Ship Seraphine, but then we fell, and he got all caught up in the wheel."

She held up her little arm to show me a crayon-shaped bandage.

"The captain went down with the ship. You'll be okay." I gave her boo-boo a nose nuzzle. And then we sat there. Not fighting.

Finally, she said, "I heard Mom on the phone with the bank this afternoon."

"Like about a bill?"

"About something called a loan. For school."

I swallowed hard. They would have to be madder than ever before to borrow money to send me somewhere. It didn't feel real, but then again, I'd never seen my little sister this upset before. She climbed out the window.

"I'll tell them you're back and asleep in a little bit. I hope it will be better in the morning."

"Do you want them to send me away?"

She reached back into the window and hugged me with those little chicken wings.

"Not today, Helen."

CHAPTER 19

FIFTH PERIOD IN THE ANTI-GLITTER UNIVERSE

GRACIE

Tuesday morning, Icing Hour

Gym first thing in the morning was sadder than I ever could have expected. I guess it didn't help that I hadn't bothered to dress or glitter up for the occasion. It felt like I was on another planet, and Coach Kline was my alien guide.

"Sasso, we don't usually allow gyming in pajamas, but I'll give you a mulligan. How you holding up?" he asked, handing me a piece of paper.

"Went over the new schedule with my moms at breakfast and did a little pre-crying in preparation for this morning."

"Solid," he said.

"I'm reminding myself that at least my lunch period is the same."

Only when I scanned the paper Coach Kline handed me, lunch had totally changed, too.

"There were two emails, kiddo. I printed the one I received right before school started."

"But I won't even hang with my bestie at lunch. If I'm thinking about traffic flows, I don't think we'll pass in the hallway once."

After the last twenty-four hours, my tear ducts had gone all Sahara, so I kind of stood there like an empty dress dangling from a hanger.

"Oh well," I said. "I need to be positive. This will blow over and Helen and I will be back together."

Coach crossed his arms and shook his head.

"I can wait my parents out and then they'll talk to Ms. Varone," I said.

"First rule of school. Once the big cheese makes a decision, the enchilada is cooked."

"That is making me confused and so hungry at the same time."

The final morning bell rang. Coach Kline blew his whistle. Kids shuffled toward the wall. He turned me in their direction for attendance.

"It is a new game. Give it a little while until you learn the rules before you decide not to play. And if things get hard today, you can always come in here."

"Thanks, Coach."

"Feel free to run as many laps as you want around the perimeter. I'll figure out how to write you an emotions pass."

I eventually made it to fifth period, which should have been lunch with Helen but turned out to be study hall in the new game. I followed my schedule to the library lounge, with the big comfy chairs and charging stations.

"Welcome to study hall, Ms. Sasso," Mr. Craft said, taking my schedule.

"Looking more like party hall. Want a cookie?" I handed over my pastry box.

"What are these?" he asked, holding one up to the light.

"Teardrops." I shoved another one into my mouth and searched for a place to wallow. That's when Isabella floated over.

"Hello friend. Gentle hugs," she said and took a cookie. "If you're eating your feelings, this is a delicious way to do it."

Madison stormed over from a circle of couches. "I get the cookies, but why are you blue?"

"Cosmically, my entire existence is being torn apart. Physically, I spent art painting blue rivers and rolling around in them," I said.

"Enough. You had your big sad. If you're here—which, by the way, no one asked me about in advance—you can work."

Madison dragged me over to the couches.

"A Girls," I said and nodded to Avery and Ashley drinking coconut water out of metal straws. "What is this place? My usual study hall is ruled by silence."

"It is a pilot program I lobbied for," Madison said. "'Collaborative study hall.' I got all the eighth graders on Cheer to request it in case we needed extra practice time. But now I'm promised a spot on the varsity squad when we start high school, so it is time for other things."

She slammed a typed sheet down in front of me and continued, "Tell us everything the school board members said after your disastrous romp through the culinary arts yesterday. Because you screwed things up beyond what I could have ever even imagined, I want to proactively address it in a social post from the Community Action Club account."

I read her post. I don't know if it was exhaustion or what, but my glitter filter totally fell.

"This is really boring. You should throw it out," I said and slid the paper back to her.

The A Girls choked on their coconut water. Isabella leaned into the circle.

"It is called persuasive writing," Madison said.

"It is like you took a social studies handout and put it in a dehydrator," I said.

"It is a bit cold, Madison," Isabella added.

Ashley actually spit up her coconut water and had to go clean up. Avery left to help. Madison stomped both feet.

"This is how you communicate in the real world," she said.

"Which is exactly why people make up worlds full of unicorns and magic and hope," I said. "How can you expect anyone to imagine a different life when you edit all the fun and joy out of it?"

I reached into my bag and found my pen topped with a ponytail and a stack of pink composition paper. But I was stuck. Working with Madison without Helen felt like betraying my bestie. My brain was convinced that we should all finish the project, though. When I sat back up, Ethan Rogers was staring at me from across the room.

"Hey," I said.

"Didn't know you were in here," he said.

"First day. Come sit," I said and turned back to Madison, who was in the middle of yelling at me.

"—serious subject, not some fantasy land—"

I held my hand up. "The good news is more people actually care about pads after the bake sale and the sit-in. But you are asking them to read. Something they aren't required to do. At least try to make it fun."

Ethan plopped down in the chair next to me.

"What would catch your eye in a post about the period products plan?" I asked him.

He flinched away like a total weirdo. "Wrong guy. Emphasis on *guy*. Maybe ask the A Girls when they're back."

"But you wore the Cuterus Uterus shirt," I started, then remembered how he'd acted at the Miller twins' house during our sleepover.

"To be funny, sort of. Don't get me wrong. I'm not saying it's a bad idea. I have sisters. And a mom. Whoa, that is weird to think about. But everyone needs to take care of themselves, right? I'm not asking the school to buy me new cleats. You know what they say, 'Catch your own blood,'" he said.

Madison had been sipping air the entire time he was talking. A good coping strategy or else she would have floated to the ceiling with rage. She smoothed out her skirt and put on a huge plastic smile.

"With your dad on the school board, Ethan, a word from you could make a huge difference," she said.

"Nah. He ran to make sure sports had full representation, you know?" Ethan said.

"A *massive* problem in suburbia," Madison said.

"Word." Ethan stood up. "Cool that you're here, Gracie. Tell Helen you saw me."

"You mean, tell her you said hi?"

"Ha. Yeah," he said and sauntered away.

"And then there were three," Isabella said. "Cozier this way. Speaking of which, let's warm this post up a bit."

"Fine," Madison huffed. "What did you have in mind?"

"Go for empathy, which I know is Gracie's superpower," Isabella said.

I squealed. "That's what I think of with you! Isabella Equals Empathy."

"This isn't a lovefest," Madison snarled.

When I thought about it, there was a letter the one time it actually felt like Madison showed me any empathy.

"Do you remember when Helen and I first came to Community Action Club?" I said.

"Yes, and I'll be sure to send you my therapist's bill for dealing with it," Madison said.

"What did that letter from Ms. Varone say?" I said.

Madison bared her teeth at me. "It just said 'Be nice.' That's it."

"Oh," I said. "So that was the problem. Being nice puts all the work on you. Showing empathy puts it on me."

"I am about to put my whole book bag on you," Madison said.

"Forget me, then," I said. "Think about the people who are against us. We could be nice and like, 'Oh, it's cool, you're right,' even though they're totally wrong. Or we could try to bring them with us—by seeing the world through their foggy glasses."

"Come on," Isabella said. She elbowed Madison and we all put on our invisible glasses.

"Smear cluelessness all over the lenses. When they say 'freebie,' what are they seeing?" I said.

"You're taking something you're not entitled to," Madison said.

"And it's definitely something you don't need," Isabella added.

Madison threw her invisible glasses off and jabbed her finger onto the paper. "Hello? I wrote that these products are necessary to attend school."

I gently put the invisible glasses back on her face.

"They can't see it. Remember, the lenses are all smeared with their own sticky fingers. We don't have to lie and say they're right, but here's why you should help us anyway. What do they see as necessary?" I said.

"I'm picturing other kinds of personal products people use at school," Isabella said.

"Like deodorant," Madison said, and she cocked her head toward me.

She wanted to hurt me, and it did hurt a little, but only because I was so over it. It struck me how weird it was that her whole deodorant thing was how we'd gotten here in the first place. Madison not accepting how someone could be different from her and be fine with it. Helen wanting to get back at her about it. I wasn't here for any of that. I wiped my invisible glasses of the school board smear and put Madison's sticky fingers all over them.

"I totally get that you would not be confident wearing my all-natural deodorant, but I'm comfortable with how I smell. I feel good about myself. You come to school your way, I come to school my way, and we can both learn. But it isn't the same with peri-ods. Let's keep noodling," I said.

Madison gave me a low growl, but then said, "Toilet paper. Helen said something about it at the school board meeting and yesterday with Ms. Varone."

"Perfect," Isabella said. "Let's try that, but in a less yelling way."

We kept going back and forth together for ten minutes, my pen flying across the page so fast that I smacked myself in the cheek with its ponytail a few times. When we were done, Madison typed it at one of the library terminals, even though I told her it would be way more powerful as a series of threaded gifs or a reel of us acting it out:

Come in close. Make sure no one is spying over your shoulder. Now imagine: You are on your way to class and get hit with the worst stomachache. You make it down the hallway in time to slip into the bathroom. But there is no toilet paper. You burst out of the stall and jump into another. No toilet paper anywhere. That's because it is your responsibility to bring your own toilet paper to school.

The bell rings. You're late for class. You need the toilet paper to be a student, but you don't have it. Maybe you can't afford it, maybe you forgot it, maybe you're embarrassed to ask your grown-ups about it. Time is ticking, you're missing class. You remember there is emergency toilet paper in the nurse's office. In a locked cabinet. But you don't have a pass to the nurse. You don't know if other kids have already had emergencies like you and used up that toilet paper. And you're going to have to talk to the nurse all about why you need it. Oh wait, the nurse isn't in our building today. You get to tell the teacher, the secretary, and the principal you need toilet paper. How do you feel?

We've decided as a society that bathrooms are stocked with toilet paper and soap. Everybody poops (hey, didn't we read that book in kindergarten?) so we all understand you need to be able to wipe your tush, wash your hands, and get back to class. We need to do the same for people who menstruate. By the end of eighth grade, that's nearly half the students in our classes. Half the students who need pads to attend school as much as all of us need toilet paper and soap. We don't choose to menstruate, like none of us choose to poop. It is part of who we are as humans. If you don't think of keeping the bathrooms stocked with toilet paper as kids scoring freebies, ask yourself: What's the difference for pads?

"That's annoying," Madison said. "I like how we're not asking for people to do anything but think and feel. I still want to add the fundraising point. What if I go completely rogue and secretly ask my dad to buy the pads without telling the PTA?"

"What about next year when you're at a different school? Who pays then?" Isabella said. "Think of it in terms of this post. We don't stop wiping our butts if we don't fundraise."

"Fine. After yesterday's debacle, I want to show this to Ms. Varone before I post."

Madison went up to Mr. Craft. There was lots of finger pointing. At each other. At the clock. At their watches. And then she came back to us.

"Come on," she said, throwing her bag over her shoulder.

Isabella and I followed.

"Where are we going?" I asked.

"You're coming to the office. There's only ten minutes left so I told Craft it would be better if we all went to lunch after this."

"But they don't give passes during the last ten minutes of class," I said, confused.

"Those rules don't apply to people like me," Madison said.

I was still processing that statement when we found Ms. Varone outside her office door.

"Principal Varone, good to see you," Madison said, trying to hand over the draft post.

"I'm on my way to a meeting," the principal said, but Madison held firm. Ms. Varone rolled her eyes but finally scanned the page. "A poop post? Really?"

"It is an empathy entry point," Isabella said.

"Which may be better left for next year given everything that happened. You have two options, Madison. Forget you ever showed this to me and post it, or I have to submit it for formal approval in the district communication—" Ms. Varone said.

But she didn't finish her sentence. She must have heard the telltale click of the PA system. The one she controls. Usually. Except while Ms. Varone was talking, Larisa had walked past us, into the office, locked the door, and turned on the mic.

CHAPTER 20

REWIND

HELEN

Tuesday morning, aka an infinity between Gracie and me

When I was sure everyone was gone the next morning, I headed to the kitchen. I couldn't remember the last time I was that hungry. The only problem was that Mom sat at the table. She should have left for work much earlier.

"You okay?" I said, pulling my headphones down.

"Taking my personal day." She pushed my chair out, sipping her coffee.

She was so still and serene. It was worse than the muffled arguing I'd fallen asleep to the night before. I slipped into my seat and found a plate in front of me. Two over-easy eggs for eyes, triangle toast nose, and a bacon smile with a glass of milk.

"Figured you'd need a good meal."

My mouth watered looking at the plate, but I didn't want to give her the satisfaction of watching me eat it. Turning that thought over in my mind, I wasn't even sure what it was connected to. What would me not eating the eggs prove? I put the paper towel on my lap, picked up the fork, and didn't look back.

"I used to love it when my mama would make me face food,"

Mom said. "She usually did it on my pancakes. I did it for you, too. You remember that in preschool?"

I wasn't sure if she was talking to me or for herself. And I definitely did not remember her making anything like this for me ever.

She didn't wait for me to answer. "But that was before Seraphine. Some things are easier with one child, but only by a little."

We were both quiet while I finished my meal. Then I said, "We didn't do it, by the way." I was ready for a fight. Honestly, I was looking forward to it. But Mom kept skipping on down memory lane.

"You know the first time I got a call to pick you up was in preschool? At four years old you'd tackled someone because he knocked over your friend's castle. And while I'm in there apologizing like you'd tried to burn the place down, they also tell me you're reading and doing math years ahead of what was expected. And they're showing me your papers, these complex sentences and ideas in your baby handwriting. I asked them what do I do, how do you reconcile these things?" Mom stopped and took a long drink from her mug. "Do you know what they said?"

"Give her a pirate ship to command," I said.

"No," Mom said.

"An entire armada," I said.

"They said, *Treat her like the kid she is.* Even if she has the intellectual capacity of someone much older. That was good advice because it can be hard to remember that the little face using examples from Greek mythology to argue against doing her word-study homework is still ruled by seven-year-old emotions, or the ten-year-old who intercepted our bank statements to show me how I could save for a family vacation just wants to meet her favorite cartoon characters."

It hadn't mattered anyway. I still had to do my homework. We never went on vacation. She may have gotten that advice, but I'd never felt the effects. She probably would have loved some go-getter kid like Madison or maybe a cheerful kid like Isabella, but she got me. And all she seemed interested in was being not bothered by me.

"What about a thirteen-year-old? How should she be treated?" I said.

"Well, what about her?" Mom said. "I still can't hold her to the standards of an adult, but I also can't excuse her decisions as a child. I did that for too long anyway."

"So maybe trust her . . . with a pirate ship," I said.

"Not letting this pirate thing go, okay. I trust her to command a ship as I would an adult, but I limit her choices as I would a child. One ship stays at Darlington, but it is never in trouble again, not even for talking out in class, not even for wandering a hallway. And the other sails for Sage Academy."

"We can't afford it."

"It may mean we never retire, but rest assured the application is complete, the loan is secured, Dad and I are united. All that is left is to bring you there for an in-person meeting and to hit send on the tuition transfer to secure your spot for ninth grade. The truth is we can't afford it, and we can't afford not to send you."

I had no comeback for any of that.

She'd never spoken to me like this before. Almost like an equal, but an equal who couldn't be trusted with herself. The idea of never getting in trouble for anything, not even for speaking out of turn over the next month—she knew that was impossible, but she was putting it on me. Like I had any decision in this under the rules of war she'd constructed. All I could do was drink my milk as my heart screamed a warning, pounding on my chest with both fists, that something real had changed, and I begged my heart to hush about it because I wasn't sure what to do next.

My schedule hadn't changed, but none of my classes seemed right, even the ones Gracie didn't have with me in the first place. Each hour that I slid through a different door and into a different chair was a new opportunity to remind myself that *nothing* would be my salvation. Say nothing, do nothing, question nothing, and we'd be fine. While she would have been starting her new study hall, I plodded through the lunch line, leaving a Gracie-size space between me and the next person.

"Grilled cheese with extra cheese . . . Mozzarella sticks with cheesy dipping sauce . . . French onion soup with toasty cheese topping. Ms. Costello, are you all trying to break my heart in that kitchen?"

Before the chef could reply, Ruth Miller jumped in front of me.

"Two grilled cheeses, please," she sang like a little angel. Then she turned around and rolled her eyes at me.

"You're sitting with us. I'm even buying your lunch," she said.

"Totally unnecessary, but thank you." To be honest, it felt good to know someone was thinking about me after the morning I'd had.

At the table, Larisa piled her papers so I could have a place to sit.

"Sorry, need to be a little asocial today," she said.

"As opposed to every other day?" Mary said.

"Rude," Ruth said.

"Ugh, I'm so sorry, Larisa. It was a reflex to you lobbing a juicy meatball in front of me," Mary said.

I did not want to imagine meatballs or any other food in the air for a long, long time. I nibbled the outside of my sandwich first, so I could save the gooey center for when things got sadder. Right about now, Gracie should have been inhaling her dessert and telling me about whatever madness had befallen her in health.

"Helen, get out of your head," Mary ordered. "It is too crowded in there already."

"Will someone make sure that Gracie doesn't choke during lunch? Like if she gets too excited," I said.

"Gracie is a human. She can eat. Oh, wait, is this a feelings talk?" Larisa said.

"I hope not . . . but what if she's all by herself and has to eat alone?" I said, my pulse quickening.

"Isabella will be there. Calm down. She's your friend. Not your ward," Ruth said.

"Very supervillain of you," Mary said.

I didn't share my next thought. What if Gracie liked hanging out with Isabella more than me? I was embarrassed to even think it. No way I was rappelling into that cavern of fears with only two slices of bread and some processed cheese food in my stomach. In fact, it was the kind of thought I couldn't imagine unpacking without Gracie.

"I'm getting a new ninety-six-color eye shadow palette. Everyone needs to come over this weekend for makeovers," Ruth said.

Larisa shook her head. "Debate tournament. Helen, join debate. Then I won't have to be partners with Mark. He wears bow ties."

"Tell her to join the tennis team," Coach Kline said, suddenly standing over us.

"I didn't know you played," Mary said.

"Because I don't," I said.

"Everything copacetic over here?" Coach asked without actually waiting for us to respond. "No straws? No food flying today? Good."

Then he got listening face. Chanting coming from the hall, getting closer. When the sound reached the lunchroom, a line of boys marched in. They wore matching white T-shirts with something scribbled on the front. And it wasn't so much a chant as a call-and-response.

"*Catch your own blood!*" Jasper yelled, turning to walk backward to lead the parade.

"It's on their shirts, too," Mary said.

The words were written in black marker—like we didn't even deserve stencils—around a dancing blood drop holding a mop.

"Does that even make sense?" I said.

"Can you chumps at least figure out the basics of human plumbing!" Mary yelled, jumping on her chair.

"Settle down," Coach Kline demanded over the chants, which were still echoing through the cafeteria.

Larisa stood up. "Coach, can't you do something? This is clearly about the issue we've been working on."

He cupped his hands over his mouth and shouted, "If a single piece of food rises above eye level, each and every one of you will be running laps before school for a week. Capisce?"

The silence was deafening. Then someone slurped a juice box. With a straw. The spell broke and everyone went back to talking and eating. Except for Larisa, who was still glaring at Coach Kline.

"What about the shirts and that chant?" Larisa said. "That was totally offensive."

"What about your shirts yesterday?" Coach asked. "These boys have words, albeit dumb and offensive words. Your shirts had reproductive organs." He weighed his hands back and forth like the scales of justice.

"They're the ones with all the power. They get to start food fights and not get in trouble. Their parents decide how the budget is spent. All the money we get for debate is less than the cost of a few lacrosse uniforms," Larisa said.

"I'm not the person making those decisions, but you've got to ask yourself, why was it okay for you to wear—" Coach Kline started.

"Bespoke and bejeweled Cuterus Uterus shirts," Mary broke in.

"Those are the ones. While you think they shouldn't get to wear—"

"The offensive serial killer scrawl?" Ruth snapped.

"If these things are the same, I am *done*," Larisa said.

"Ten minutes left of lunch and there is food on plates. Let's get it in bellies. Wells, I will see you on the kickball field seventh period," he said, backing away.

Please, not today. I turned to ask Larisa if there was any chance debate club met during school hours, and more specifically during seventh period, but she wasn't there.

At least her body wasn't there. A few minutes later, her voice was all around us, coming over the PA.

"The right to free speech is not absolute. You can't say anything you want if it will cause violence or if it isn't true and will harm someone's reputation. That last one is something many people in this school should be familiar with. But I would go even further. When you think about the things you hear and say at this school, I want you to remember the power behind the people saying it."

I got up, threw my bag on, and dropped my tray in the recycling bin. At the door, Coach Kline tried to stop me, but I waved him off. In the hallway, Larisa's voice echoed and enveloped me until I felt like it was lifting my feet right off the linoleum.

"Telling me to stand up for myself doesn't mean much if the people I'm standing up to have all the power and I have none. The teachers won't act because the principal won't act. Because the superintendent won't act. Because the school board members who hire him won't act. Because the community who votes for them won't act. Our school system is supposed to educate us, but we have no say in it. We are sitting in a fluorescent-bathed, low-key nightmare with no way for things to get better.

"My speech alone won't save me from a system I can't access in the first place, but my speech is all I have. Anyway, Ms. Varone is busting in, so I want to ask all of you: What should we say here? Whose voices should be elevated? Was anyone listening to Gracie yesterday when she talked about imagining something better? Making fun of people advocating for what they need cannot be the future. Imagine how Darlington would work for YOU to feel safe and healthy and valued. What are YOU willing to do to demand that change?"

I got to the office as the mic clicked off. Gracie, Madison, and Isabella were all standing around the assistant's desk in the outer office. I slipped my hand into Gracie's and watched Larisa take a seat at the talking table, and Varone clicked the mic on.

"This infraction will merit disciplinary action. If you were thinking of doing anything similar, I suggest you think again," she said.

Varone started yelling at Larisa the minute the mic clicked off. Every line on the office assistant's phone lit up at once. Madison stomped her feet back and forth so hard I was sure she'd break something.

"You, you, you!" she yelled at me and Gracie when she turned to go.

"Larisa is special, and so are you," Isabella said and gave me and Gracie a simultaneous side squeeze. Then she handed me a paper.

"The poop-based argument. It is art," I said after reading.

"Let me go make sure Madison doesn't have an aneurysm," Isabella said.

"They won't listen," Gracie said gently. "Even when you literally steal the microphone."

It was all part of the same larger problem. Getting the answers right without anyone caring if you're learning anything. Not trusted to go to the bathroom when you needed it. Putting conformity and accomplishments over relationships.

"We just need to get through the next month, have fun all summer, and figure next year out next year," I said.

"What if our parentals' separation discussions have extended to the summer?" Gracie said.

"What do you mean?"

"I didn't want to upset you, but now that we're split . . . my moms have been talking to your parents about how you always get me in trouble, which is completely ridiculous, but . . ."

Gracie kept talking, but I hardly felt like I was there in that hallway anymore. We'd spent the last four years sidestepping the rules to do our own thing. But I couldn't see how that could go on for the rest of this year with Varone watching our every move, let alone the four I was staring down at the high school not in class with her. This system would not let me be me. It would not let me be with my friend. That wind that was supposed to be pushing the pirate sails at my back felt like it was sneaking, squeezing around my throat.

I didn't know if it would have turned out this way if the system had been built to include girls from the beginning rather than throwing us in as an afterthought. But I did know it was time to stop talking and start doing. There was one action from all our brainstorming that I kept coming back to that was big enough, bold enough, would interfere with pooping enough, that it just might work. No one would read Madison's post. We would make them feel it.

I felt myself cutting the rope that tethered that Darlington pirate ship to the docks.

It was time to activate Operation Crocheterus.

CHAPTER 21

CROCHETING OUR WAY TO CHANGE

GRACIE

The next Monday after school, Lobster Tail Hour

Team Tampon made big things happen over the next week. Turning the trouble dial to a Level 5 with the sit-in hadn't worked, and neither had kicking it up to Level 7 with Larisa taking over the PA and getting her first detention ever. The jocks mocked us during lunch. Our empathy post on the club's social account got like twenty views (probably half of which were Madison on different phones and computers). In the halls, she snarled at one of us from time to time without coming up with some other plan. So, when Helen suggested we crank up the Action Meter to Level 9 by replacing all the toilet paper rolls with crochet uteruses? Everyone was ready.

We quietly organized a grade-wide secret crochet circle for the plan. Helen's crochet uterus lock design made its way to a bunch of kids the Millers recruited, and they shared it with their friends. Isabella provided the raw materials and made how-to videos. It seemed like combining feeling fed up with the powers-that-be at school with a fun activity was the secret sauce for change. And I mean, really, is there anything better than rage crafting?

The afternoon before the big event, Helen used her computer brain to draw up a mapped route of all the school bathrooms, and I put on my most posh delivery outfit to collect everyone's creations: Brown camo sweatshirt dress, blue-and-black cheetah-print jeggings, Ugg boots, and big cross-body tote. Once I had the homemade uteruses, I'd meet Helen and Michael F. in his backyard for the final assembly.

I loved playing reverse Santa, going to people's houses and demanding cute things from them. Larisa was my first stop. She met me outside her apartment building.

"I had enough yarn and fury to make three," she said.

"There is plenty of 'womb' in my bag for them," I said.

The unthinkable happened. Larisa laughed. "It was a fun way to spend the time while I've been grounded for the whole PA thing."

"How has the fallout been?"

"Lunch detention was incredibly productive. I might send myself there again. At home my parents are so busy with work they couldn't do much. My dad said I was grounded, but I had to implement it."

"Self-grounding. Now, that is innovative."

"I don't know if this action will make a difference, but it will certainly make a statement people can't ignore. I'm sick of the nodding."

"My bladder is the size of a pea, so I definitely could not ignore toilet paper being replaced by yarn art. Give it up for Tiny Tinkles." I put my hand up for a high five. Larisa shook it and went back inside.

Then I skipped to Isabella's house, where I found her twirling and marching on the sidewalk. Someone would have to call the hospital if I ever tried to make my knees go that high.

She waved to me and threw the baton up in the air. When she stopped and put her hands on her hips, I realized she had zero intention of catching it. I pumped my legs faster than Sunday night, when the first butt to hit the couch is granted supreme control of the remote.

The late afternoon sun was blinding, but I set myself underneath a twinkling in the sky and held my hand up. The baton fell like a javelin and landed right in my sweaty paw. My mouth literally fell open and didn't close until Isabella took the baton back.

"This baton has not hit the ground in two hundred and twenty-three days. That is how much I believe in you, Gracie Sasso," she said, handing me the tiniest crochet heart before skipping over to her porch. I plopped myself down on a bench swing and gave it my all. Until I knocked into the side of the house.

"That's supposed to be more of a relaxing swing, Gracie. Take a look at these," Isabella said.

She sat down next to me and showed me a pile of uteruses crocheted in our school colors. On some she'd sewn smiley faces.

"It has been so cool hanging out with you. Clearly, you are truly talented at this stuff," I said.

"I've got lots of ideas, but I always worried they were too out there. Like every time they make us do lockdown drills, we should end the day by spelling out 'Enough' with our bodies. Or at lunch, if we wanted to get rid of the factory meat they serve, we could hold a meat-free BBQ showing everyone how delicious it can be."

I really loved eating disgusting cafeteria meat, but I loved Isabella's ideas more.

"You need to bring this all up with the club."

Isabella shook her head. "It comes from Cheer. My approach is to get everyone excited and involved. But Madison runs the club, and even though we're on the same team for the same sport, she comes at life from a totally different direction."

"From the bowels of hell," I said.

"From a desire to wow. All the boxes checked. Her team will always have the most trophies. You can't really measure fun. I'm glad she got tapped for varsity next year. We'll have a little breathing room on JV." Isabella jumped down from the swing and resumed twirling.

"Want to catch it again?" she said. "Things can only get more interesting the darker it gets."

"I normally do not turn down the chance at a dusk-related head injury, but I've got an herbalist to check on. Ciao ciao!"

The route to Michael F.'s house took me a block away from Aunt Carmella's house. A teensy detour was in order. I found her setting up for a night planting, so I grabbed an apple from her picnic basket and splayed out on the grass under her weeping willow.

"Is gardening in the dark new-weird or ancient-weird?" I said.

"Maybe you're the weird one," she said, sitting back on her clogs glittering with metallic stars. "Everyone knows you plant potatoes by moonlight. And don't fill up with the apple. I'm making pasta and potato soup for dinner."

"That is the most deliciously carbtastic name for a meal I've ever heard, but, alas, I'm in the middle of revolutionary activities with Helen and Michael F."

"What about the sad one with the blond hair?" she said.

"Madison? She's not sad, she's mean," I said.

"Sadness is like a lasagna," Carmella said.

"No. Stop."

"Some layers are red with anger—"

"You're straight-up making these sayings up at this point," I said.

"All sayings are made up, but fine, maybe that one needs a little more seasoning," Carmella said.

"Besides, we're leaving Madison out of the revolution from now on," I said.

"Why?" Carmella asked.

"Because she'll say we're doing it wrong. Although we didn't tell her about the last thing and it sort of shredded my life. Anyway, she thinks you should only play by the rules," I said.

"What do you think?" Carmella asked, stabbing her trowel into the dirt.

"Helen's plan is to show how the rules are unfair," I said.

"When did you change your name to Helen?" Carmella said.

"Very funny," I said. She knew I was a feeler, not a thinker. But if I was? I didn't know if showing people that the rules were bad was enough. Like, when someone tells me my outfit is hideous, they really can't be surprised when I put on something even worse. Telling someone what's wrong is totally different from showing what's right. And I would almost certainly put on something worse out of spite anyway.

"All I'm hearing are reasons to include Madison," Carmella went on. "Go talk to her. Give her a chance to surprise you."

"You always assume people want to be surprised. Some of us want the world to go as it always—" I stopped myself. Because that wasn't what I really wanted at all. I wanted the whole world to change. And first, I wanted the school to change for everyone, including Madison.

I sat up and watched my aunt attack the dirt. "I'll make you a deal. I'll give Madison a chance if you give Mommy a chance to surprise you the next time you talk."

Carmella sighed. "Maybe she's not the one who needs to surprise. But okay, you have a deal."

I figured while I was going for it, I might as well go for it. "And you have to agree to help me when I need it. No questions asked. Give me a chance to surprise you."

That got her laughing again. "I don't know if that is a great or terrible deal, but I'm definitely taking it. Now, come inside for a minute. I went to the bakery today. You should take some sfogliatella to the revolution."

A box of lobster tails couldn't hurt. Especially if I was telling Madison what we were up to.

Madison swung her front door open and snapped, "What?" when I rang the doorbell ten minutes later. She was sporting a messy bun with pencils, pens, and highlighters sticking out of it.

I told her about Operation Crocheterus. She was not pleased. She did not surprise me. Honestly, she didn't seem too surprised by me, either.

"Seriously, what else should I expect? I was done after the food fight. I was super done after Larisa's little stunt. Now that I know what you're doing ahead of time, I feel like I have to report everyone." She crossed her arms and let out a big huff.

"What will that get you? The people in charge, even your bestie on the school board, aren't interested. This is either important enough to put yourself out there or it is just another line on your résumé," I said.

"What will crochet uteruses get you with the board?"

"They can't be ignored because . . . poop."

"Have you thought for a second about how all your nonsense hurt my advocacy? You're destroying something that really matters to me."

Honestly, I hadn't thought of any of it in that way. Once she said it, though, I thought about what I had gone through during the sit-in. That the same kind of prank I would have reveled in a month ago broke my heart when it hurt our project. I didn't know what to say.

"Forget it. Let's focus. Our empathy post—" Madison said.

"No one looked at it."

"We'll pay five dollars to promote it. We'll get someone to share it on the town parent page. I'll even add the gifs you wanted or make a video. That is more likely to get people to the next school board meeting than crochet uteruses. Now we have evidence the pads are being used. I've had to refill the PTA box every single day. And I'm reading all these finance papers, trying to come up with a budget argument. Help with the numbers instead of getting into more trouble?" Madison said.

Her desperation had clearly reached nuclear meltdown levels if she was asking me to do math. Madison knew that was Helen's realm.

"It is bad enough I'm talking with you separate from my best friend. I won't torpedo our awesome plan, too," I said.

She narrowed her eyes at me. "Your plan or Helen's plan? Can you even think for yourself enough to answer the question?" And before I could answer, she slammed the door in my face.

I ran all the way to Michael F.'s house, arriving a huffing, puffing, teary mess. Whatever Madison thought of me did not matter. I could think for myself. I was my own person. I turned into the backyard and went straight for the tent.

"What happened to you?" Michael F. asked.

"One-seventh-life crisis," I said, breathing heavy.

"Make it one-eighth, okay?" Helen said. "I'm not losing you before we both turn a hundred. This will cheer you up. Mike has been entertaining me with all kinds of Gracie facts."

"Dude," Michael F. said.

"Anything interesting?" I asked.

"You always know the exact shade of any color, to the point where sometimes he'll research them when he's at the hardware store with his dad, and you're always right," Helen said.

I dropped my bag and myself onto the tent floor without

responding. I mean, that was basically a marriage proposal. But a complete dissection and analysis of every word they shared would have to wait.

While I spilled out the crocheted uteruses, my travel craft box, and the lobster tail pastries, Helen unrolled a massive drawing of the school with boxes listed for all the bathrooms.

"I really should have asked what this was all about when you invited me to my own backyard," Michael F. said.

"We're utero-locking the toilet paper rolls," Helen said.

"Fallopi-jam?" I said.

"Ovarian-nono?" Helen said.

Michael F. looked more confused than ever, so I said simply, "We're reverse TPing the school."

"And tomorrow is the ideal target because it is Sloppy Joe Day," Helen said.

I thought Michael F. was going to push his glasses right into his beautiful brain. He picked up one of the crochet uteruses and held it up to the camp light. "So you're taking all the toilet paper rolls out . . ."

"And putting adorbs crochet wombs in, yes," I said. "The cutie-pie ovaries fit over where the roll holder would snap in." I turned to Helen. "Even though I know what we're doing, I feel like I'm still going to order sloppy joes at lunch."

"Same," Helen said. "We should share through the crochet whisper network that girls might want to use the bathroom in the morning if they also make terrible cafeteria meat decisions and don't want to get stuck."

"Wait. Hold up," Michael F. cautioned. "This could get you in a considerable amount of trouble."

"You don't have to do it," I said.

He shook his head. "I'm in, don't worry about that. But what about you two? No offense, but your trouble cup is already spilling all over the more well-behaved kids," he said, pointing to himself, "and this takes a fire hose to it."

"Nothing we can't handle, so let's focus," Helen said.

Michael F. sighed. "Well, if we're going to do this, we might as well be as strategic as possible. Make the switch during the last ten minutes of class when no one can get a pass so the bathrooms will be empty? Then the, um, effects will be felt the next period."

"Mike, you are a genius, no wonder Gracie likes you. Oh. No . . ." Helen said, her eyes getting real big.

My mouth dropped open again. Michael F. reached out and gently pushed my chin up.

"It's okay. I know Gracie is either going to kiss me or make me vomit," he said.

My inner squeal squealed so loud I could hardly hear myself think. I mean, can you get sweeter than remembering that?

"Now, you said something about scouting when you invited me?" Michael F. said.

"You know all those knots you were tying?" I asked.

He laughed. "I even tie them in my sleep."

"Is it true there is a knot that gets tighter when you pull on it?" I said.

"Sure, the arbor knot. I tied about a hundred of them," Michael F. said.

"We need to turn all of these ovaries into arbor knots, so if someone tries to take them off, they just get tighter on the roll holder," Helen said.

Michael F. held the smiley-face uterus up to the light. "Coolest scouting badge ever."

CHAPTER 22

UTERO-LOCKING MY HEART

GRACIE

Tuesday afternoon, Intestinal Distress Hour

The next day everyone met at my locker before my study hall and Helen's lunch. A very well-timed bout of insomnia meant I'd spent the night rearranging the rhinestones on my cat burglar onesie from LA PUZZA to SANGUINA.

"Should I ask?" Helen said.

"It bleeds," I said.

"How do you say 'perfect' in Italian?" she said.

"It is pronounced 'Helen Wells,'" I said and blew her a kiss.

We'd organized into teams over text the night before and worked out how many uteruses everyone needed to cover their assigned bathrooms. We handed out the arbor-knotted beauties from my locker.

When the bell rang, everyone went to their assigned rooms as usual, except for Isabella, who decided to launch from the nurse's office.

In study hall, I watched the clock, the teacher, the door, the clock, the teacher, the door, until Mr. Craft asked, "Ms. Sasso, are you all right?"

"A little parched," I said and poured my entire water bottle down my throat.

"I know what you're doing," Madison hissed, but I had no time for her.

In all honesty, I had to pee so bad it felt like my bladder was raging against the other organs in the mosh pit of my belly. But I couldn't ask for a bathroom pass. That wasn't the plan. Not until there were only five minutes left of class.

Then I shot my hand into the air.

"Another hydration issue?" Mr. Craft said.

"I need to jet to the ladies."

"Wait for the bell," he said, invoking the stupid policy, that this one time was very useful, of not letting us go to the bathroom during the last ten minutes of class.

"I'll turn the corner into a potty, then."

He looked at the clock and then squinted at me. "Fine. Take your bag with you. Come back tomorrow a little less disruptive and a little more distributive."

I cackled as loud as possible because I did not have time for this man's math jokes outside of math class, and I ran out the door. The plan had been to check around all spy-like, but I really did have to pee and there couldn't be anyone else in there with two minutes left, so I ran to the bathroom, yelled to make sure no one was in there, peed thirty gallons of water, used the toilet paper, then removed the toilet paper and replaced the roll with a crochet uterus, attaching the ovaries to each side of the tube holder. I busted out of the stall and did the same for the other three. Then

I taped our "Period Equity Now" flyers to each of the stall doors. Sliding back into the hallway as the bell rang, I finally paused to breathe and looked for my friends.

Ruth and Mary were walking the other way in their office-aide smocks and gave me a double wink. Twin power! I found Isabella shoving rolls of TP into her locker. She whispered without turning to me, "Helen gave me a thumbs-up in the west hallway. We're all good."

"And now we wait," I said.

"Until one of them has to take a dump," Isabella said and gave me a wicked grin. "By the way, first time I've said 'dump' in this context. I wonder how we'll know if it worked."

It didn't take long to find out.

After the bell rang, Isabella and I sat at the table closest to the door in the cafeteria. Soon we heard the squeaking of sneakers. It was faint at first—whoever it was must have tried a faraway bathroom—and got louder and louder until it reached our hallway. I slipper-stepped to the door. Isabella followed. Helen came into view from around the corner. And then came more eighth-grade girls.

Jasper. One of those lacrosse dudes from the Millers' house. The one who hit me between the eyes with a spitball. One of the boys Helen told me paraded around the cafeteria, chanting.

Maybe I should have thought it was fitting to find him stuck, but it didn't matter. There were so many people who felt like him that any one of them could have benefited from having to think about what life is like for other people.

He ran into the boys' bathroom across from the caf. There was a bunch of banging and then he ran back out, spewing a series of curse words that under other circumstances I would have made note of for later use. Finally, Ms. Varone came marching down the hallway and pulled him away from the door.

"Jasper, explain yourself," she said.

"I need to drop a load, and there is no toilet paper anywhere. Just these weird sock things."

Ms. Varone called to make sure no one was in the bathroom and pushed past Jasper, only to reemerge a moment later.

"Looking for this?" Ruth Miller said as she walked down the hall in her office bib. She was holding up a single square of single ply.

"Ruth, you know about this? You're an office aide, for goodness' sake," Ms. Varone said.

"The reflective tape over my heart doesn't make me less of a person, Principal Varone. Also, this is dumb. Meetings? Bake sales? Protests? You know what we need. Put the pads in the bathrooms already."

There was a chorus of yeahs, and how-do-you-like-its, and I-am-so-sick-of-dealing-with-these-jerks.

Ms. Varone turned to me and Helen. "I pulled on the 'weird sock' and it wouldn't come off. Arbor knots?"

"Always be prepared," Helen said.

"And on Sloppy Joe Day no less. Ruth and Mary, go to the art room immediately and get me some sharp scissors. Jasper and any other students in need, you may use the bathroom in the main office." Ms. Varone whipped out her walkie-talkie, alerted Mr. Allen to the situation, then hung up and turned back to us.

"That is school property you've taken. I want it brought to the supply cabinet immediately, and you will each be hearing from me later today. You two, Gracie Sasso and Helen Wells, go to my office now," she said.

"That's our speech. You can't punish us for speech," Helen said.

"It is vandalism. For a second time. To think that you're asking for an honor system to use the bathroom when this is how you behave in the bathrooms." Ms. Varone shook her head. "You say you want to decide how the school spends its money, but it is just more prank nonsense the minute there is an obstacle in your way."

"Your nonsense of the ten-minute bathroom rule is what allowed us to get the pranking done," Helen said.

Varone looked like she might lose it. We had made our point and couldn't afford to break her. I didn't know what Helen was thinking.

"This is how you girls think we achieve change? I have a school to run here. Access to a bathroom is a health and safety issue," Ms. Varone continued.

"Um, that is the *very literal point* we were making," Isabella said.

Ms. Varone stopped talking. She straightened her blazer. And then she gave us one of those terrifyingly blank smiles that adults save for when they're about to obliterate your hopes and dreams.

"You see these two as your role models?" she said, pointing to me and Helen. "A few days ago, they were put on separate schedules to stop causing trouble. Do you want me to do the same for you and your friends? No? Not sure? Let's make things crystal clear. Ms. Wells and Ms. Sasso are both suspended. Out-of-school suspension. I will tell the high school to keep you apart when they're putting together the freshman sections for next year. I will work with your parents to make sure you are never together again. Now, go sit at opposite ends of the office while the secretary calls them to come get you."

By that time Ruth had brought the scissors and Ms. Varone handed them out to teachers she'd called on the walkie-talkie. She went to start cutting without even looking at us again.

Helen and I walked through the crowd, past kids telling us good job, that they had our backs, that we all would make it happen. But the person I needed to hear from had stopped talking.

"I guess we should have known this was a possibility," I said.

"A probability."

"We keep fighting."

Helen stopped. "I don't think so."

"Come on, Helen, they can't win and let these sportsball kids do whatever they want when no one can spare a few dollars for us."

Tears welled in Helen's eyes. "They're putting me in all honors classes next year."

"OMG, of course they are!" I said. "You'll be teaching the classes by the end of the year. But I don't know why that means we stop fighting."

"You don't understand—"

"Don't get me wrong. I hate being without you. This week has shown it is awful and doable and made me really value the time we do have together. We'll still have the bus, after school, and cutting class. I hear that is practically its own sport once we get to high school."

"No, because they'll send me to Sage Academy now for sure."

"They won't."

"Mom said one more screwup and I'm done. My pirate ship is sunk."

It was finally sinking in that Helen and I had entered this day through the same door, but would leave it through exits miles apart.

"We didn't have to do this, Helen."

"We did. I hoped maybe we could make something change for real. Or maybe even accomplish something, enough to get everyone to leave me alone? Or maybe it was all because I finally found something at school that matters. I'm so sorry, Gracie."

And she left. She ran to the end of the hallway, past the office, through a group of fifth graders walking outside for gym, and right out the doors of the school.

Helen was gone.

CHAPTER 23

RAINBOWS RAINING FROM MY EYEBALLS

GRACIE

Friday morning, Iced Coffee Hour

It was our last day of suspension. I'd gotten texts from half the girls in our grade, but not a peep from Helen. I needed to talk to her, to process what happened, and to share the new plan I was working on. But it felt like she had disappeared, or maybe like she had disappeared me. I hoped we'd find each other back in school Monday, even if we were split up.

"Was there a problem with the eggs?" Mommy asked me.

She cleared the nearly-full plate from my bedroom desk. I was grounded, more than I'd ever been grounded before. No leaving my room, not for the kitchen to bake, not to eat with my family in the dining room, and definitely not to sneak out at night and find my best friend. My parents even stuck a baby monitor inside one of my unicorns, and I couldn't find the will to moon it or anything.

"They were good. I'm just not hungry."

"If you prefer bagels or donuts, don't get suspended from school." She had taken three days off from work to "watch" me.

"I understand, Mommy."

I thought she was leaving so I got up to find my rainbow marker set and put the finishing touches on my plan.

"And you will clean this entire room today," she said.

I bent down to pick up a paper that had dropped on the floor, and some stuffies I'd been cuddling with as I cried myself to sleep each night. I went to my bookcase and straightened all the spines. There was nothing else to do, but she didn't leave.

"I need to go to the pharmacy. It should only take a half hour. Can I trust you here alone?" Mommy said. Then she laughed. It was a dry, loud laugh, and I hated it.

I turned to face her. "It will be fine."

She pointed a finger at me. "If you leave this house—"

"What?!" I yelled so loud I scared myself.

Mommy gasped and covered her mouth.

I went back to my desk like nothing happened and started coloring in my plan.

"You don't raise your voice to me," Mommy said, totally raising *her* voice.

"Correct! Bingo! I don't yell at anyone. Maybe I should," I said, not looking up from my work.

"You have no right to get this angry."

"You can't teach me my whole life that my feelings are valid and then change your mind when they make you uncomfortable. Maybe you would take me seriously if I yelled."

"Say something worth listening to and stop acting like a maniac if you want to be taken seriously," Mommy said, but she choked on her own words. "Not to say we don't take you seriously . . ."

I pushed my plan into her hand.

IMAGINATION + PEOPLE = POWER
* Ruby Red: HELEN WHERE ARE YOU?
* Sunset Orange: Gossip reels, but for really boring people
* Jelly Yellow: Madison + Snake Bread = Victory
* Glitter Green: Everybody chills slightly to get it done
* Electric Blue: School Board Meeting—Unique Voices Edition
* Power Pink: Pads-In-Bathrooms!

"I have a lot of important things to say. Stuff like this. It's my plan to fix things. I know it won't save Helen and me, but at least it will do something that matters and get pads into the bathrooms at school. You know I can think, right?"

Mommy gently wiped her eyes. I took the paper back.

"If I'm translating this from Gracie-speak correctly, it looks like a really good plan."

"Just because I say things in glitter and rainbows and makeup and fart jokes and cupcakes doesn't mean those things I say matter less than what other people put in spreadsheets. Which, by the way, is a truly weird word."

"But honey, those things really do determine whether people take you seriously or not."

"I'm taking myself seriously. That is a good place to start. It would be much more dramatic and satisfying if I stormed off right now. As you know, I do not have a car or license and have never figured out the bus map. I need to finish color-coding this plan, and then I need for you to drop me off at the *Cambridge County Herald* on your way to the pharmacy."

"I can't. You're being punished. This isn't a vacation."

"Who goes to a newspaper on vacation?! I'm doing what you want. I'm finishing something. I literally put my head down like Mama is always saying and figured this out. Please call her."

And we did.

"I was wrong, Mama," I said.

"Thank you for finally apologizing, little love," she said.

"Oh no, I'm not apologizing. I'm making things right. This should never have been about following the rules or burning all the rules until they're unrecognizable. It should be about showing people a better way to be. Not just saving money or saying money doesn't matter but showing how our school will be better off if we take care of kids' needs first. We need everyone to imagine what that better future will be. I, me, Gracie, am the perfect person to get everyone together even if this whole thinking experience is very dehydrating. Sometimes you need someone who doesn't always act as expected or else how can we think of anything but what we're already expecting? I am blowing my own mind here. Anyway, I can help bring a little joy, a little fun, and a lot of unpredictability to help people see something they never imagined before." No hemming, no hawing, no putting myself down, no apologizing. I was behind my own self. It was terrifying. It was glorious.

"Actually, this sounds pretty good," Mommy said, a little too surprised.

There was silence on the phone. But I knew it wasn't to bring up an unfinished tree house or mosaic. It was thinking silence.

Finally, Mama said, "It makes a lot of sense. I've got to get back to work, but I'm proud of you. Obviously, you're still—" I hung up before she could finish.

I turned back to Mommy and said, "Let me do this, and then I will sit in my room like a gorgeous, grounded Rapunzel for all of eternity, and all I will ask of you is some luxurious leave-in conditioners."

"I don't know, Gracie."

"Also, fighting with you makes my insides feel like they're melting, so can we please stop."

I dove into her arms and cried. Hard. Like ugly whole-body sobs. Everything was a wreck because of me and Helen: School, the parentals, freedom, the period-product plan. We were also the people to fix it, and if we did it right, maybe we could get done what would have been impossible before the wreck we created.

"Will you help me?" I asked her. "The first step in my rainbow plan is getting Helen back. Will you text her mom about meeting us at the newspaper office?"

"Shhh, shhh, shhh," Mommy said, stroking my hair. "All right. How much trouble could you get into at a newspaper office? But remember we don't know what Helen is up to."

CHAPTER 24

SALTINES

HELEN
Friday morning, aka my future

Sage Academy was indeed a school made of many bricks. Stacked, interlocking, and mortared into a peppy prison to lock me away from my best friend—any friend—and into pleated skirts and knee socks. What was most annoying was that it was nice, and all the people were nice. I should have been thankful to go there.

Rachel, the girl giving me and Mom the grand tour on my last day of suspension, was wearing all the pep, even an ascot emblazoned with the school's logo.

"This is the cafeteria, or 'Munchie Hall,' as I like to call it," Rachel said. "It's got all the usual stations, like salad bar and grill, but most of us live for the froyo machine with unlimited toppings. You can eat here even if you're a day student commuting from Darlington."

"Are there Menstrual Munchies?" I said.

"Sorry?"

"Nothing."

I was absolutely broken, but there is only so much a non-lobotomized human can stand. This pixie-in-plaid had already led me in the school's fight song and told me the history of every garden bench we walked by. I couldn't even be annoyed, because she was doing exactly what we'd asked her to do: show me what life would be like when my parents double-mortgaged our lives to send me to this high school.

"Want to stop in? Gummy bears will so be my downfall," Rachel said.

"We'd love to," Mom said.

No more protesting from me. My only regret was not having accepted my fate sooner.

Rachel led us into the enormous cafeteria, big enough to fit three of Darlington's lunchrooms and filled with sunlight from massive stained-glass windows. Pockets of girls chatted. Others sat reading or typing on laptops. I'd gotten the lecture on how freeing uniforms could be, but all I saw was a place for me to get lost.

Rachel offered to get our frozen yogurts, which defeated the fundamental purpose of a choose-your-own-fixins bar. Mom wanted to visit the health food selections and told me to snag us some seats. I wandered for a minute, then stopped at the end of a table with one girl in the middle.

"Cool if we sit here?" I said.

"Sure. Are you on a tour?" she asked.

I nodded. "Do you like it here?"

"It's my fourth school in four years and they're giving me a diploma so I can move on with my life. So, I love it. Seriously, though, the academics are tops, and there's a lot less nonsense than other schools."

"I am the nonsense," I said.

The girl laughed and packed up her bag. "Not here. Simple, safe, no-drama education means things are simple, safe, and drama-free. You get a lot of peace in exchange for the conformity, like unlimited froyo."

Mom and Rachel sat down, chatting away like they had been friends for years.

"Where is mine?" I asked as they dug into their sundaes.

"Brenda told me—"

"You're on a first-name basis?"

"—that you're a little lactose intolerant. I got you saltines instead," Rachel said.

And that was how it went. Mom and Rachel gorging on ice-cold gummy bears and cookie crumble over frozen yogurt while I gnawed on dry crackers.

"A few more things to cover," Rachel said, finally turning back to address "Brenda" and me. "Every girl is required to play or assist with a sport each trimester. My three sports were fencing, chess, and softball."

"What if you don't like to sweat or play sports or do things in general?" I asked.

"Helen, you're so silly. The school makes every accommodation so every girl can join three teams," Rachel said.

"Even—" I said.

"Everyone," Rachel said, louder, and as her voice rose her smile got bigger. "And of course, you'll complete a service project."

"I have one of those," I said, feeling oddly excited to share.

"Great. What is it?" Rachel asked.

"Do you have period products in the bathrooms here?"

Mom coughed. "Not while we're eating, Helen."

"I'm missing something," Rachel said.

"That's the project, period equity," I explained.

"This is an all-girls school. We're familiar with the phenomenon," Rachel whispered. "Helen, your test scores are off the charts. Sorry, peeked at your file in the office even though I'm not supposed to. Obviously you're a wreck, which is no reflection on you, Brenda. Even the teachers who clearly hate you—which is all of them, in case you were wondering—think you're brilliant. You will *thrive* at Sage Academy, and then go out and build our alumni brand. Don't ruin that success before it starts by yelling about P-E-R-I-O-D-S."

Rachel stood up and put her hand on my shoulder. "I also had a colorful record when I started. You need to leave everything that brought you here in the past. Good luck, Helen. And Brenda, I will see you on my Instagram feed."

Then there were two. Mom and me, staring across an abyss strewn with rainbow sprinkles and cracker crumbs, with nothing to say. She sucked on her teeth. I rolled my eyes.

"You don't realize it now, but you are worthy of all this," Mom finally said.

"Odd word choice," I said, folding my saltine wrapper into a boat.

"You'll meet new friends, like Rachel, when you go to school here. You will find things to do that are worthy of your beautiful mind."

Worthy. Showing abilities that merit special recognition. She'd said it twice in less than a minute.

"I found something worthy, Mom."

She wiped her fingers carefully on a paper napkin. "Don't you think I can see it's just another one of your stunts? Making people smell like skunks, covering school board members in red paint, switching toilet paper for yarn . . . I gave you a choice."

"It wasn't a real choice," I said. "You set me up so I'd have to go to this place so you don't have to deal with me."

"For once could you assume that I'm not out to get you? That Dad and I are actually trying to do what's best for you?"

I knew she wanted me to think that they'd sacrifice anything for me, but that was some fairy-tale nonsense where she got to be the hero.

But maybe I wasn't totally right about casting her as the villain, either. Although her not even offering me a bite of that frozen yogurt had to bring her pretty close.

"I'll take it under advisement," I finally said.

She sat back and gave me a look Principal Varone would be proud of. "You want me to trust you with life decisions? Then it is time to decide who you are, Helen."

"I just want to be the same as I've always been. It feels like everything is slipping away, changing. Let me coast through high school, let me and my bestie stick together, let me worry about the future and whatever else once I figure out how to get through each day."

"Do you think that's what Gracie wants for you?"

I choked on my next protest. Stopped in my tracks by Mom Logic. Brutal. Of course that wasn't what Gracie wanted for me. She'd want me in all honors classes, joining teams, even going to this ridiculous school if she thought it was the best for me. And I'd want that for her.

"No, but I know she'd want us to finish the project, and she cares about why it is important to me."

I finally told her the full story about getting my period early and not having a pad. She looked like she wanted to crawl under the table, but then she reached out and took my hand in both of hers. They were warm and strong and somehow smaller than mine now. A tear plopped on them. I was crying in an upscale reform-school cafeteria, and I did not care.

"It isn't just me. This stuff matters to every kid who has had to hide a tampon on their way to the bathroom or who checked their butt a thousand times a day for the outline of the pad. And also, about all the girls and other kids who are sick of it," I said through actual blubbering. There was liquid coming out of my eyes and my nose. There was even drool.

"Sick of what? I don't understand," Mom said.

For the first time, I wondered if it wasn't just that she didn't want to deal with me. Maybe she really didn't have the first clue what I was going through. Maybe neither of us knew who I was.

"How can you not understand?" I said. "You've been my age."

"Then, I forgot, so tell me. We didn't talk about this stuff in my family. At school it was just slides of terrifying diseases. I thought at least I was doing better with you."

Then she leaned in like she wanted to know everything I had to say.

"*This*. We're sick of not being listened to and taken seriously. Mom, so many kids. All you see is anarchy and stunts, which, hello, correct, but think about it. We got twenty kids to give up their plans on a beautiful spring week to learn to crochet uteruses."

I felt a gentle tap on my shoulder. It was a security guard.

"Perhaps you would like some fresh air," he said.

"We're having a moment here," I said. "A uterus wrapped in a maxi pad wrapped in an eternal mother-daughter moment!"

He backed up like I was holding a spear to his belly, but Mom pushed me out the door all the same. I wiped my eyes. My cheeks felt raw.

"Snot is running into my mouth. It is really salty."

"You always did love eating your boogers. So, I already know we need to check in with your pediatrician at the next visit about your period coming early so she can answer all your questions. What else are we talking about here?" Mom sat me down on a bench.

"There was an order to the madness. I'm not saying it was planned, but as we got more into our world—the Helen and Gracieness of it all—more kids got involved. It was like the fun was an entry point. And the wilder the stuff was that we did for a purpose, the closer we seemed to get to some good. Somehow getting suspended was the closest and farthest we were from making change at the same time. In math you would call it—"

"Chaos theory," Mom said quietly. "Only you would find a dynamic system in your bad behavior."

I burbled out a small laugh. "Gracie and I need to bring it back to where Madison started, but now there's so many more people involved and willing to stand up for change. I am lost, but maybe Gracie—"

"All right."

"What?"

"You can finish your project." She held up a hand. "Don't get me wrong. You are going to this school next year. But I've never seen you this passionate about something that wasn't solely destructive."

Then she hugged me. An honest, full-bodied, two-armed mom hug that draws the hurt and pain out of you. I hadn't felt it in years. I didn't want to let go. But her phone buzzed.

"Work?" I asked, blotting my eyes for what I hoped would be the last time in the next thousand years.

"No, it's a text from Gracie's mom. Your presence is requested at the *Cambridge County Herald*'s office. And would you look at that," she added, and held up the screen for me to read.

Brenda, our girls may be onto something.

CHAPTER 25
TIME TO MAKE THE NEWS

GRACIE
Friday afternoon, Katsup Hour

I walked into the newspaper office like I owned the place. If I had a little more time for ensemble assembly, I'd look like I couldn't be bothered to own the place. My red trench, power jeggings, and a pair of faux snakeskin pumps I snagged at a thrift store even though I could barely walk in them would have to do this time around. At reception, I asked, "May I speak with the education reporter, Claudette Kang?"

"Who should I say is here?"

"Tell her that *justice* has come to call," I said over my rhinestone cat-eye sunglasses.

Then I took a seat on an awful couch to wait for what felt like ages—until the front door flung open. I jumped to my feet in case intrepid reporter Claudette Kang had raced back from a hostage situation or burning building to meet me. But it was Helen who ran in and hugged me.

"You smell like tears," I said, pulling back to inspect her puffy eyes.

Helen sniffled. "I've been legit blubbering. There were waterfalls of snot. No wonder I gave it up in elementary school."

"I've been crying, too," I told her. "And I've been trying to get in touch with you all through suspension. We clearly have more telepathy work to do over the summer."

"I thought about calling you a thousand times, but I didn't know what to say, plus I wasn't allowed to use the phone. Standing here I still don't know what to say. I've had my headphones on blasting emo music for three days straight."

"I've been listening to death metal for three days straight . . . but at a low volume . . . subversive," I whispered and handed Helen my plan.

She scanned it and smiled at me. "Love that I was red. Are we here for orange?"

I filled in a heart next to the first line. "Yes, Ruby Red is done. Now Sunset Orange: Gossip reels, but for really boring people."

"It looks awesome, Gracie. What do you think about adding a Tantalizing Turquoise before the school board meeting?"

I squealed. "Hello, get in my eye shadow palette! What did you have in mind?"

We sat down on the terrible couch together and she explained.

"We ask Ethan for help. Maybe that sounds weird or whatever, but his admittedly awful dad is on the board and he wasn't one of the boys doing that stupid chant in the lunchroom. Maybe him talking to the board would make a difference," Helen said.

She looked almost like herself again. For a split second I thought about saying *for sure* and ignoring the turquoise elephant in this room. But Helen was my best friend, not just for the spray-can cheezapaloozas and fart hotboxing and wildly experimental makeup tutorials. She was my best friend because

I loved her, and sometimes when you love someone, you've got to tell them the boy they have a crush on is moldier than a sentient blue cheese.

"We asked him already, me and Madison," I said gently.

"Oh," Helen said.

"The only reason Ethan wasn't chanting in the caf was because he was in study hall with us, being a total weirdo who said the same line from that dumb chant. He wouldn't talk to his dad. Oh, but he did want me to tell you that 'I saw him.'" Which I was realizing I hadn't done and actually not feeling that bad about.

"I keep thinking some part of him cares because he wore the Cuterus Uterus T-shirt to that first meeting," Helen said. "And honestly, because I thought he sort of liked me and I sort of liked his jacket. Saying it out loud sounds like I'm making excuses."

"He's the excuse," I said. "Of course he likes you, you're gorgeous, brilliant, hilarious, fearless, and deserving of every pastry proposal in this town. But, like . . . don't you also deserve more than a boy who just sort of shows up, wearing various shirts and outerwear?"

"Yeah, I do. Thank you for seeing me even when I can't see myself," Helen said.

We were interrupted when a woman dressed in ratty jeans and a blazer with elbow pads came out of the elevator and walked up to us like she really owned the place.

"I'm looking for Justice," she said.

"Aren't we all," I said.

"My bad." She turned for the reception desk.

I hobbled on those heels to get in front of her. "Sorry, I'm new to this clandestine stuff. I'm Gracie. This is Helen. We're here *for* justice."

Claudette Kang crossed her arms over her chest. "I need to grab lunch. Walk with me."

It was then that I realized dealing with the press should be done in the most sensible footwear possible. We had to run to keep up with Claudette as she cut through parking lots and back alleys to reach her deli. In between twisting more ankles than I even had, Helen and I told her about the period equity plan.

"Great angle," she said. "Give me a call when it's done. I'll do a piece, get a quote from you two, and ask the governor's office when they'll do it statewide."

She handed me her card and ordered ham, egg, and cheese on a roll with extra butter on the eggs, two ketchups, and three salts. It was disgusting. I loved her.

"The thing is, we can't get it done without your help," I said.

She shook her head and wiped cheese from her cheek. "Not how this kind of story works. I could spend all my time spinning my wheels chasing stuff that kids, parents, whoever are trying to do and never publish an article. You need another hook if it's not done."

"I've been reading all your work in the county paper and our local *Darlington Dispatch* articles about the school board," I said.

Helen gasped. "You've been reading outside of school?"

"I'm telling you, the death metal has really inspired me to do some rage research. Anyway, this is what I've found. Our school board only does something when it is covered in the big county paper. Teachers, parents, kids—even the mayor—can shout all they want, and the town paper can write about it, and people can post on social, but if they won't look bad beyond our town, the school board doesn't care," I said.

"You've read all my articles?" Claudette said, taking a swig of coffee.

"Even from your days as an intrepid student at the *Daily Collegian*—loved the Fashion Week coverage, by the way— through to the last time you wrote about our town when the old superintendent tried to cancel Halloween last year," I said.

Claudette laughed. She crumpled up her garbage and basketball shot it into the can across the room.

"See, that story had another angle. A candy grinch versus a real-life witch. I would have loved to talk to her one-on-one, but her public comments were pretty good. The story actually got picked up on the national site by our parent publisher for a day. You need that kind of action for press before something happens when you're competing with the other fifty small towns I've got to cover."

Helen grabbed my arm at the word *witch* and hadn't let go.

"What if I could get you an interview with the witch?" I asked Claudette.

"Don't promise something we can't deliver," Helen said.

"Carmella said she wants to support us," I whispered back.

Claudette crossed her arms like she had in the lobby. "I don't know. That story was over in the fall. But I would like to hear what she's all about. I've got a soft spot for the people boards can't stand but always listen to. When is the meeting?"

"Monday at 8:00 p.m.," I said.

"Maybe I'll take a look at things before then," Claudette said, heading for the door. "But now I've got to go back and meet deadline on a sewage treatment plant Bellville approved next to their elementary school. Godspeed, kiddos." And she was gone.

A low-key panic set in on the drive home. Things had been tense when we ran back to the newspaper office and our moms were talking on the sidewalk. Helen's mom whisked her away before we could debrief, and I drove to the pharmacy with Mommy. She told me Helen's mom kept talking about the frozen yogurt selections at Sage Academy, which, yes, critical information under normal circumstances, but not what I needed to know about the future with my bestie. I fell into a negative-thought loop about us being apart, and how whether we could figure things out depended in a lot of ways on whether our adults would let us.

And here was Mommy, able to hash things out with her sister whenever she wanted, and not doing it.

"Will you talk to Aunt Carmella?" I asked when we parked in the pharmacy lot where Carmella worked.

Mommy sighed. "I've given you a lot of leeway considering how upset you've been. Can we not do this today?"

I put my chin next to her headrest. "She doesn't even remember why you're not talking."

When she turned back to me, her eyes were sad and tired. Generally, I suggest a yellow-based concealer with a hint of brightener in such circumstances, but in this case, it was best to lean into it. I patted her head and Mommy gave me a sad chuckle.

"Oh, she remembers. You know, Gracie, being an only child is a blessing and a curse. It means you don't know what happens between sisters. Sometimes it is better to not deal with things," she said.

"But I do know best friends," I insisted. "Just give Aunt Carmella a shout-out when you're in there. Like a 'Hey girl,' totally casual. It doesn't have to be this whole tragic opera thing. Just a first step."

Mommy got out of the car. I followed.

"Gracie, what are you doing?"

"I just want a snack."

I threw my arms out and felt the star power of the automatic doors bursting open for me. The air conditioner blew my hair back and gave my heart a jolt. Rounding the end of the baby formula aisle, I met Carmella's gaze from the dispensary counter. She slid off her reading glasses and waited for us to approach.

"Dropping off, picking up, or do you have a concern you want to discuss?" she asked.

"Picking up, for Sasso," Mommy said.

"You know, you can just set up delivery, so you're never forced to come in here," Carmella said as she rummaged through the *S* bin.

I waited for Mommy to say something, anything, while Carmella rang up the medicine. But there was the bag. And there was the change. And there was Carmella going back to work.

And I was so annoyed that two people who loved each other could maybe actually be with each other if they only talked, so I rang the little bell on the counter.

"Service! I have a concern to discuss," I said in my most devastating faux British accent.

Mommy put her hand on my shoulder, but I spun out of it.

"What are you doing?" she whispered.

"Solving everyone's problems but my own apparently," I said as Carmella returned to the counter.

"What do you recommend for a ridiculous feud?" I asked.

"Time," Carmella said.

"Tried it. Left a huge scar. What else?" I said.

"Truth," Carmella said.

"Unavailable—" I said.

"What if it is available," Mommy said. She stepped next to me.

"You remember?" I said.

"Our mother's pizzelle recipe. Carmella told me the cookies were soggy. That they were a disgrace to Ma's memory. That I was a terrible cook, and shouldn't be allowed to make her recipes anymore, especially the ones with garlic," Mommy said quietly.

Carmella sighed, but she didn't look away. "I should not have done that. Let's have the peace between us."

"I can't let it go. I've spent most of my life trying to deal with my emotions instead of sweeping them under the rug, and today Gracie reminded me that if I'm going to tell everyone else to be in touch with their feelings, I better do it myself when it counts."

Carmella shifted in her stilettos and looked behind us—a line was forming.

"Okay, okay, you came, we're moving on now—"

Mommy grabbed Carmella's hands across the counter.

"That was always our problem, moving on instead of dealing with things. They build up until they are too heavy for anyone to carry. Carmella, I was so little when we lost her. You had her songs, her cuddles, her history, her time. Those recipes were all I had. Those recipes and you. Saying I shouldn't make the cookies was like you telling me I shouldn't have any connection to her."

Carmella walked away. Then she came out of the dispensary door. When she reached us, I felt as if we'd entered a vacuum where nothing made sense and everything was possible. And then Carmella grabbed Mommy and hugged her. And cried.

"I took my pain out in teasing you," she said. "The pain of missing her. I put it on you, and it tore us apart."

Mommy cried, too. And then I cried. Because maybe that level of drama is baked into my soul.

At home Mommy was excited to tell Mama all about making things up with Carmella. Or the extremely early stages of starting to make things up to be more realistic. Part of me was happy to be out of the line of parental anger and wanted to lie on the couch and eat cheese, but another part wanted to keep this problem-solving train rolling. Having seen the result of a three-year sister feud fueled by sweeping things under the rug, I decided the Gouda would have to wait. I mean, where did it have to go, anyway?

"I really need to see Helen," I said to my moms after dinner.

"Still grounded," Mama said.

"But I'm telling you instead of sneaking out. Growth?" Then I hugged Mama, and I didn't let her go until she hugged me back, for real. And then she was the one who didn't let go.

Mommy finally hugged both of us. "It has been a big feelings day. Want to go for a drive together while she talks to Helen?"

Mama looked back and forth between us and laughed. "We're going to need a bigger car battery to get through high school feelings, aren't we?"

I didn't need a jacket when I headed out onto the street. It felt like rain was coming, but not for a while, and I liked the way the night weighed on my skin. I stuck to the sidewalks this time, not wanting to deal with any dogs or sprinklers or tents. The neighborhood was quiet—until someone shouted at me.

"Hey!" Michael F. called out from his garage.

"Are you actually allowed inside your house?" I asked, meeting him in the driveway.

"Mom is making me camp out again. Get this, Gracie. I didn't meet the requirements for compass . . . or tying knots." He smiled so big that I saw his teeth for the first time ever.

"Oh, Michael F., that is the most precious thing I ever heard in my entire life. Do you want me to go in there?"

Michael F. full-on laughed. It was light and sweet and made his eyes sparkle.

"I'll tell her you almost brought a school down with your knot-tying prowess," I continued and turned toward his front door, but Michael F. had reached out and was holding my hand in his.

"I missed you at school," he said. "We got a stern talking-to, but you and Helen . . . there has been a lot of shouting next door. I mean, there usually is, but it's been more urgent this week."

"Thank you for caring."

He put his free hand in his pocket.

"I wanted to give you this."

I was flattered, of course, but it didn't seem like the right time for an engagement ring, but also not the right time for . . . wadded-up note cards.

I took my other hand back from his to uncrumple them.

"You dropped them at the school board meeting. It's a great point. I'm sorry you didn't get to share it in front of the board," he said and shoved his hands into his pockets.

Ugh! I couldn't believe I'd thought he was doing something silly like asking to spend the rest of his life with me, when he was doing something infinitely cooler like paying attention.

"You saving these cards means a lot. I put together a plan to basically save the universe, or at least get pads in the bathrooms, but things are weird between me and Helen. She doesn't know the full extent to which I cheated on her with Madison."

I told Michael F. about trying to make peace with Madison and working together and telling her about the uterus locks ahead of time and that it was literally eating me up from the spleen out.

"That's not how cheating works, Gracie. Also, not how spleens work, but that can wait. Having another friend isn't cheating on the first friend. It is just having another friend," Michael F. said.

"We collectively can't stand Madison, so that part is definitely cheating."

"What about individually? Do you as a person hate her?"

"More like I don't like her and I want to be her and I want her to care about what I think all simultaneously."

"Maybe you need to have your own opinion about her, and as weird as it is, to me it sounds like something friendish," Michael F. said.

"Are you trying to tell me I'm not replacing Helen with other people but becoming more of my own person? What's happening? Michael F., catch me," I said, dropping to the ground. "Call the doctor, I'm having an epiphany!"

"You don't need a doctor," he said.

"Then call a doctor of philosophy," I said. But Michael F. didn't call anyone. He pulled me up and faced me. Really close.

"Is this when we kiss, or you make me vomit?" he asked. This time he didn't push up his glasses. He slid them off and into his pocket and pushed back his hair.

I ran.

"That part comes later," I yelled as I sprinted toward Helen's house. "Official friendship business now!"

Helen was already waiting for me at her window when I got there.

"Was that you yelling?" she asked.

"I wrote the social post with Madison."

"I know."

"No, like, we sat down and worked together."

"Gracie, I didn't think Madison came up with that gorgeous rendition of a classic pooping analogy on her own. It had heart. Of course you wrote it."

I blew out a raspberry and slid down into the grass.

"I thought you would be mad because I was working with Madison. I tried to exist in this weird middle world between you two that made me feel like I was having heartburn at every meal. And all of you were putting me in that position because you cared more about your way than a way that worked," I said. And I was surprised because my voice was rising. A lot.

"Are you yelling at me right now?" Helen said.

"I believe so. I'm sort of yelling at everyone today," I said.

"I'm here for it. And I'm sorry. It wasn't a weird middle world, though. You were finding your own way. The Gracie Way."

"Now, I would buy that on a T-shirt." I said it like a joke, but I meant it. Helen needing my brain felt amazing. Like she was seeing more of me than ever before.

"And now we're finally doing it with your rainbow plan. I'm a little embarrassed, though."

"For being so fabulous—please Helen, it will be a lifelong issue, so as Mr. Rogers would say, learn to deal with it now."

"No, for like a minute, or multiple minutes that reoccurred from time to time, I got upset and jealous of Isabella."

"But we both know her. While I'm worried about Madison, you're worried about Isabella? Classic."

"I thought you had study hall and lunch together and she's cool so you would get close and abandon me, and you're the only person I've ever let get close in the first place, and this—this is why it is a no on the feelings front."

I took her beautiful face in my hands and squished her cheeks until they turned into a fishy mouth. "Your parents can send you to high school on Mars. I could become the most popular girl in town. We could take up separate hobbies—shudder. You will always be my best friend because you love me for me, and I get to experience that massive heart of yours that will burn the world down with love whenever you're ready to release it."

"It is a little schmaltzy," Helen said through tears.

"Personally, my teeth hurt," I said.

"I have the salty snot raining down my face again."

"Eat it up, girl."

Helen wiped her face on her sleeve. "Are we good?"

I nodded. "Do you want to talk about what's been happening with you? Mommy shared some suspicious froyo deets, and Michael F. said there's been shouting."

"There is always shouting . . . but yeah, Sage Academy might be a done deal, or they might never let me back for speaking of unspeakable lady parts over that froyo."

"Now you're making me want to go there."

"I have a short window to make things right. I'm all in with you."

"Perfect," I said, pulling out my plan. "Time to get Madison back in: 'Jelly Yellow: Madison + Snake Bread = Victory.' I will make her a big, braided bread loaf in the shape of a snake eating its tail."

Helen held her hand up. "Let me get this one."

"But she super hates you."

"Madison can deal with the hate after she sees I found a way to pay for this plan. I mean, Gracie, we'll save these knuckleheads money." She handed me a binder and went on. "After we got home from the paper, I got on the district website. Once I read through the budgets and contracts, it all came together pretty quick."

"Oh, Helen, did you . . ."

"Indeed. I did recreational math, and we're about to find out if it was enough."

CHAPTER 26

APOLOGIES

HELEN

Saturday morning, aka a good time to skip town, but here I am

Madison lived in one of Darlington's biggest McMansions. It had a pool and a pool table. This was the kind of house where your parents made sure you were wearing nice clothes before they dropped you off to play. At least my parents did, before the invitations stopped. That was back in elementary school, and I was in no mood to be here again now.

Gracie rang the doorbell. She looked like she might vomit.

"You're not nervous, are you?" I asked.

"Me? No. Putting one smart dragon and one super-smart dragon into a gilded cage together to argue over something they both care about? What could go wrong?"

The door swung open. Madison's white tennis dress, gold snake armbands, and blond braids gleamed at us.

"We have a video doorbell. I heard everything you were saying. You can go now. Also, I am a super-smart dragon, too," Madison said.

"Interesting that you assumed you were only the smart dragon," I said. Wow. Would I ever be able to stop myself?

Madison slammed the door in our faces.

Gracie found the security camera, pushed her hair back, and went into soliloquy mode.

"Dear Madison, super-smart dragon of the mount. We come bearing tidings of mathematical wonder," Gracie said. I popped the binder out of my bag and held it up behind her.

"For in another land, an equally super-smart dragon, with a different but also valuable skill set, has investigated the last five budgets of the magical school masters. And she found where there is gold to be plundered."

We bowed. I didn't straighten up until the door opened again.

"Get in here before you embarrass me in front of anyone else," Madison said.

I turned to find a group of power walkers had stopped behind us.

"We bid you adieu, fair maidens, adieu," Gracie said, doffing an imaginary cap as she backed inside.

Madison sat on a couch in her foyer, which happened to be the size of a hotel lobby. I expected to eat pie upon pie of crow, so it was time to get on with it.

"I'm sorry, Madison," I said, plain and clear.

That got her to glance up from her cuticles.

"Sorry for what?"

"I'm sorry for only going all-in on maxi pads after I was directly impacted. I'm also sorry for not including you in our other strategies. You were the one to research the issues, find the solution, and go to the board. We all should have worked together. I didn't respect what you had done and what it meant to you," I said.

Madison got up. She paced, fast, her sneakers squeaking on the gleaming tile floor with each turn.

"Fine, I accept your apology," she finally said.

"Great, now we can get to work," Gracie said.

"What about your apology, Madison?" I said.

Gracie gulped. Madison stomped. I didn't care.

"Girls in the club like Larisa and Isabella have amazing ideas. Most girls in the school have amazing ideas. You can do something I never could—work with anyone who will help you get the job done. But being a leader means making sure everyone is really included. Everyone pushes the change together, not pushing you while they stand behind," I said.

"None of that matters anyway. I am done with middle school clubs. They're a waste of time. I'm already making connections with high school projects." Madison stormed off into the house. We followed. She stopped at her dining room table. It was covered with battle plans, assuming the goal of war was entry into the National Honor Society.

"These are the different clubs I can join next year and their connections to various cliques. And these are the teacher advisers I'm most likely to want an influential letter of recommendation from." She stopped pointing and put her hands on her hips. It was beautiful and disgusting. It was so Madison.

"You're playing the same game in high school?" Gracie said.

"This is a road to accomplishment. You two couldn't even hold it together to do one thing. I am talking about a lifetime here. It all starts now."

Gracie and I shook our heads.

"Tacky," we said in unison.

"Being successful is not tacky," Madison said.

"This?" Gracie said, waving her hand over the plans. "Tackier than bad lip liner."

"Whoa," I said.

"Tackier than a furry manicure," Gracie said.

"OMG," I mouthed.

"Enough," Madison said.

"Tackier than '90s eyebrows. And I say this as the Queen of Tacky," Gracie said. "Accumulating things is not the same as accomplishing them. Like, I have accumulated thirteen unicorn stuffies, but I have only accomplished meaningful friendships with three of them."

"Finish accomplishing this thing that would mean a lot to so many kids, including kids we haven't even met yet," I said.

"Kids that haven't even been born yet," Gracie said. "Madison, that is as close as you can get to performing magic."

"I'm the one who told you about this issue, don't you think I know that!" Madison said.

For a second I tried to convince myself that we didn't need her. We had the math, Larisa's words, Ruth and Mary's schmooze, Isabella's enthusiasm, and Gracie's glitter brain.

But Madison had the gravitas, plain and simple. The board trusted her, Varone trusted her, teachers trusted her, other kids trusted her. She existed in this system, and now we could give her the data to make the decision unavoidable and the noise to make it urgent. She could make the ideas + people = power on Gracie's plan work. I decided to go big. Real big.

"Play you for it," I said.

"What?!" Madison said.

"You're in that outfit already. One game of tennis. You win, we leave," I said.

"After raiding your fridge, of course," Gracie said.

"I win, you work with us to make it so a kid at Darlington has to go out of their way to not find a maxi pad. Fair warning, I play with my dad on Sundays."

Madison steamed. "You know I'm on the country club tennis team."

I, in fact, did not know that.

"I was invited onto varsity tennis in seventh grade. I only turned it down because I am fully committed to Cheer."

Another fact I was not aware of.

"My dad built me a court last year."

I followed her pointer finger to look at a whole honking tennis court in her backyard next to the pool.

"All useful data points, but I'll still beat you."

Madison sized me up. The cutoff shorts, the free coding-camp T-shirt, my saddle shoes. But she had to also see the thing I had that for some reason she still didn't have. Total confidence. Even when I didn't deserve it.

"This is dumb. Tell me about the budgets anyway," she said.

"Do you remember at the last meeting when they were talking about the vendor contract renewals?" I said.

"That's when I wanted to launch myself into space," Gracie said.

"Those are the ones. They were trying to find which companies would give the school the best price on paper products, to save us money and be efficient. So, you could have the nurse go to the pharmacy to buy bandages, the custodian go to the grocery store for TP and paper towels, etcetera. Or you could buy all those products bundled from this one company. But! They're not actually saving the school money compared to the price of things if we went to a store to buy them. It's just that *bundled prices* are cheaper compared to these companies' *individual prices.*"

Madison's grumbly expression suddenly cleared. "The overpriced bundles the school buys from these companies cost less than their even more overpriced individual products," she said. "But the point is that it's all overpriced?"

"Bingo. I found that you can cross out certain items, or substitute for the bundles they offer. From what I've read, the town is paying almost $2 for each of those ridiculous, individually boxed and shrink-wrapped maxi pads. We can supply all the bathrooms with normal pads for that money."

"You can prove it?" Madison said.

"There are so many numbers you need to be a computer or crawl into Helen's brain to get them all, but even I understood the final math she showed me," Gracie said.

Madison tapped her foot. We had her. I could feel it.

"Whatever," she said.

"No," Gracie shouted so loud I yelped. "We are not whatevering, Madison. You care."

"For my résumé. That's what you threw back in my face, right?" Madison said.

"Because that was shame time. Didn't work. Now it is truth time. You care because you know how messed up it is that they don't listen to you at school or those board meetings—you of all people should always get heard. Except you're not. You do the sports, the grades, the do-gooding—and none of it matters in the end," Gracie said.

"When I was really upset last week, my dad said if I were a boy, I would run this town. But since I'm not, it's better to get through high school and get out. I'm sick of it."

"Does this mean you're in?" I said.

"Yeah, I'm in. I already realized I was being a jerk a little while ago, but sometimes it is hard to swim out of that spin," Madison said.

For the first time, I understood Madison. Thankfully, Gracie was committed to keep us moving.

"Let's go chat it out. The kitchen would be best because you have that great island to work on, and I really need to get in your fridge. I bet you have fancy cheese!"

CHAPTER 27

ALL ABOARD THE GLITTER BRAIN CHANGE TRAIN!

GRACIE

Saturday, Fancy Cheese Hour

Within minutes, I was deep into a wheel of Brie and explaining my approach to glitter braining. Madison had rolled up her extremely sad high school domination papers and lugged a flip chart out of the coat closet.

"The key concepts are one, need for change; two, desire for change; and three, funding for change," she said, writing.

Helen nodded. "You did one. I did three. Gracie researched her butt off for two."

Madison laughed. When Helen and I didn't join in, she stopped.

"You're serious? Sorry, Gracie, it's just . . . you're not known for that kind of thing," she said.

"I contain multiples, Madison," I said.

"Multitudes," Helen whispered.

"Those too," I said.

Madison handed me her marker. I flipped to the next page of the chart and drew a shooting star, a smiley cupcake, and a heart with *You Are Beautiful* written in the middle.

"What is that?" Madison asked.

"It's something to make this horrendous white easel easier to look at," I told her. "A blank page is almost as terrifying as a blank cookie." Then I gave Madison the gist of my press research and our discussion with the county reporter.

"Impressive. I go to all those meetings, and even I didn't realize that. Okay, so when I'm brainstorming—"

I shook my head.

"—when I'm *glitter braining,*" she corrected herself, "I start with the end point and move backward. Here, I would say, 'Thank you from the bottom of our hearts to the Darlington Board of Education for recognizing the need for period equity and approving funding to provide pads in all school bathrooms.'"

"Perfect," I said.

"Now we work backward. The point before that would be the actual vote—" Madison said.

"Ewwww. I hate moving backward. It makes me nauseous. Let's put what you said out there as our starting point instead," I said.

"But it hasn't happened yet," Madison said.

"Like a statement?" Helen asked.

"I'm thinking a video," I said.

"Oh no, what are you going to say?" Madison said.

"No, what will you say?" Helen said, pointing a finger in Madison's face. "This all started with you. It needs to end with you."

I used my director hands to frame the shot. "Madison sitting at the table, looking fab, a box of pads positioned just so, maybe a menstrual cup casually leaning up against them. Talking only as Madison can."

Madison jumped up from her chair. "It is lying. I won't be part of it."

"Lying is such a mean word, Madison. At worst this is future truthing," I said.

"Remember Varone said make it seem the obvious choice, like something they were already planning. And our reporter friend said to let her know when it was done," I said.

"This, what you're suggesting, isn't what either of them meant," Madison said.

"We know research, logic, persuasion, and yarn arts alone will not work on this board's inertia. That's like when you're on a roller coaster—" I said.

"I know basic physics, Gracie," Madison said.

"Good. The board is on a roller coaster, flying over the hills with their hands in the air, and we're in line wondering, 'When is it our turn?' And you are the brakes that stop them from going around again, and they lurch forward in their seats, which freaks them out a little, but then they get out because it's time to give someone else a chance and they can go get some snow cones."

If this kept up, I might end up teaching physics myself.

Madison stretched for a moment and then pounced, throwing her hands down on the table.

"Let's do this. But I don't want to be roller coaster brakes. I want to be a boulder. And I want them to go flying out of their seats. No snow cones!"

She styled herself for the shoot. It was the exact opposite of what I would have chosen and absolutely perfect. Over her white tennis dress, she tied a red-white-and-blue silk scarf around her neck and pulled on a blue wool blazer. Next to some boxes of period products, she stood up a pocket constitution and a framed picture of an old-timey women's march.

I pressed record, Helen gave the go sign, and Madison gave the world a smile Barbie would be jealous of:

"My name is Madison. I am a student at Darlington Middle School, here to say thank you from the bottom of my heart to our school board. At Monday night's meeting, I expect our district will make this school a leader in period equity in our state by voting to make maxi pads available in all middle school bathrooms. We all know that every kid who menstruates needs access to these products in order to be safe and healthy, and our district knows how to keep the budget safe and healthy, too. This change will save taxpayers money. I hope my friends and neighbors will join us for this historic vote. See you at the middle school library Monday night."

"Cut!" I yelled. "That was wonderful."

Madison steadied herself. "Were there enough qualifiers to make it not lying?"

"Definitely not. Not enough qualifiers at all. Welcome to the revolution, Madison," Helen said and gave her a side hug.

I waited for a black hole to appear and swallow us up when those two touched. When that didn't happen, I posted the video to my page and waited. It wasn't long before there was a heart.

"Who is it?" Helen asked, looking over my shoulder.

"Ugh, just Mommy," I said. But then there was another. And a share.

"Carmella!" I screamed. I went to her feed, where she had written, *Finally, a good use of public money. Period Equity for all!*

"We should tag some big names," Madison said.

"Let's see what happens with the people we know and their connections," I said. Carmella's share was already getting hearts. And shares. And comments from women she was connected to.

About time.

How does the state not mandate this already?

This would have made such a difference when I was a young girl.

I went back to my original post. Some kids in school liked it and shared it and only a few included blood and barfing emojis. I went back to Carmella's feed. There were already thirty hearts. When I scrolled through the names, I screamed.

"Intrepid Reporter Claudette Kang liked your video off Carmella's feed," I said.

Helen and Madison screamed, too. We didn't need to tag big names. The local people we needed were watching.

"Who is the other person with a blue check?" Helen asked.

I clicked on it and screamed again. "Someone named Elisabeth Durand . . . a reporter with RCKZ News!"

"The county access station they play at dentist offices!" Madison yelled.

"OMG, my mouth hurts whenever I see their logo!" Helen yelled.

We were all yelling and jumping and scrolling. My brain felt like glitter was shooting out of my eyes, ears, and nose. This was it. This was our chance.

"What's next on the rainbow?" Helen asked.

"'Glitter Green: Everybody chills slightly to get it done,'" I said. "As painful as this is, it's time to rein in some of that chaos we caused at school and ask it to come to the board meeting. Green means go back to the beginning."

CHAPTER 28

EVERYONE SPARKLES,
EVERYONE SHINES

GRACIE

Monday afternoon, Éclair Hour

The Activities Room was packed after school on Monday. It was weird to be back post-suspension and to have fully accepted that after school would be the first time I'd see Helen. But I believed in my heart that we had even more important things to worry about, and I couldn't wait to dive into those consequence-infested waters with her.

Michael F. told me he was concerned about the room's legal occupancy limits as kids sat on desks, the windowsill, the floor, anywhere they could find a perch. I told him to have some snacks. In addition to getting the word out about the final Community Action Club meeting all weekend long, I'd found enough time to bake nibbles worthy of this amazing group.

My pièce de résistance was the tampon éclairs. First of all, choux pastry is a beast. I used the frozen kind I already had in our freezer, even though that was really it for my Sugar Stash for the year. Mama suggested I get something called a "summer job" if I wanted to replenish supplies. So now I have to see who will be hiring a fashion and baking genius in June. I'm thinking Paris,

Milan, potentially São Paulo. Mommy suggested the community pool or babysitting. Those babies will have to seat themselves for now. We still had work to do.

Anyway, once the éclairs were made, you'd think, wrap them in white fondant and be done with it. Um, no, try me being an edible art goddess who used a toothpick to sculpt each one until it looked like the tampon was being pushed out of its applicator.

Ruth devoured one and asked for another.

"They are too delicious, and they make me want to hurl," she said.

"That is the Gracie way," I said.

When we couldn't fit anyone else in the Activities Room, Madison stood up.

"Welcome to the final club meeting this year. Would the secretary please read our mission statement?"

"To do the thing tonight," Michael F. yelled from the seat next to me, cupping his hands like a megaphone.

Everyone laughed. Even Madison. He didn't have his meeting minutes notebook out. Of course, I was destined to fall for a rebel.

"I get it, thank you all for coming. There has been some chatter on socials that a few parents may complain at the meeting, so us showing up in force matters. Here is the plan for tonight. I will start by revisiting the need for this project and the finances," Madison started.

Ruth was annoyed. "Hold up. Isn't this what you guys did last time? What's the big plan? Helen? Gracie? Are we gluing the board members in their seats until we get some justice or what?"

I snaked my way to the front of the room.

"Supergluing unsuspecting adults should be its own sport in the Olympics, but we're not planning anything like that for tonight," I said. There was actual grumbling.

"As much as it pains me to say this, we need to harness all that anarchy—taking over the lunchroom, commandeering the school PA system—"

"We love you, Larisa!" someone yelled, and she turned bright purple in the front row.

"—the signs, the T-shirts, everything. We need to bring that energy to the meeting tonight. Because while it took all these kick-butt forms, that energy was really about each of your unique voices. The board needs to hear us, and they might not listen if we create too much chaos."

"Then are we standing behind you while you talk, Madison?" Larisa asked.

Madison nodded and clutched the podium. "Exactly. We'll assemble as this unified group while I do the introduction and preview the new financial research."

"And then?" Helen said.

Madison tapped her foot. A rabbit would have been worried about her ankle it went so fast.

"And then," Helen said much louder.

"Stop, it is like you are verbally pushing me," Madison said.

"I'm about to verbally tackle you," Helen said.

"And then, after I do the introductory info, I will step back to create space for each of you to express yourself in your own way," Madison said.

"And . . ." Helen said.

"And I won't pull anyone aside or make excuses if your message doesn't exactly align with mine. But please don't glue, pour paint on, or cover any board member with sticky sweets. What I'm saying is, use your voice in your own way, but *think* about how it fits into the bigger picture of what we're trying to do."

And that was it. By creating space, Madison got all the kids talking about how they wanted to make their voices heard. We spent the rest of the meeting hashing everyone's talking points out, thinking about which order might be most effective, and coming up with a color palette for our looks. I lobbied hard for red, gold, and glitter, but in the end our school colors—Sunshine Orange and Atlantic Blue—won out because most people agreed this change was really about our school community. I don't ever want to hear anything about my pastries being too sweet after that schmaltzfest.

We created a sign-up sheet following the board's pattern so no one would miss their chance to speak. It was all I could do to not list myself as "Seymour Butts" so the president would have to read it out loud. But my head prevailed over my heart, and I ended up writing "Ms. Gracielle Sasso, Menstruator, Pastry Makeover Artist, Human."

"I don't think they need your occupation," Michael F. said.

"Those are more states of being than occupations," I said. "How does it feel not taking notes, by the way?" I said.

"Oddly okay," he said.

"Will you try it in class?" I said.

"Good God, no," he said as he put all the pages together to bring to the school board as everyone was leaving the club meeting.

"I'm torn on my two-minute topic," I said. "I had prepared my note cards to talk about why the pads should be in the boys' bathrooms, too, but I really want time to show how pads are just a first step to equity."

"I want to talk about the boys' bathroom point anyway," Michael F. said. "I want to cover this nonsense that we can't see pads or whatever."

I thought back to that first meeting when Michael F. stood up not only for turtles, but people with periods, too. He kept trying to do the right thing over and over again even though no one ever sentenced him to caring.

"You would be doing all this even if I wasn't involved, right?" I said.

"Of course," Michael F. said. Then he took a step closer to me and gave me another one of those smiles with actual teeth. "I was all in even before you joined the club, but supporting you is a pretty great bonus."

"I've made a decision," I said, because suddenly it was true. "I want it all, Michael F. First, may I kiss you?"

"Um, now? Right. Yes." He turned his cheek to me as it turned a billion shades of purple.

Was I really going to say it? Oh yeah, I was totally saying it.

"On the lips?"

Ahhhhhhh!

"On school grounds? I mean, yes. Definitely yes," Michael F. said, taking off his glasses and leaning toward me.

And I did kiss him. At least, I sort of stuck my face onto his. His lips were pillowy soft, just like I'd imagined, and for a second, we were breathing the exact same air. It felt wonderful, and I knew making him hurl would have to wait.

CHAPTER 29

ACTUALLY WINNING

HELEN

*Monday night, aka I was honestly looking
forward to extra time at school*

That night we gathered for the school board meeting. Or as Gracie put it, "Electric Blue: School Board Meeting—Unique Voices Edition." If I were a jock, I would say this was the big game. But I'm not a jock. I'm a chaos monster with a chip on my shoulder who is amazing at math and has the best friend a weirdo could ever ask for. So instead of getting pumped up and ready to go, I sat on the grass with Gracie, rage-checking my budget calculations.

"Enough!" Gracie said. "What if the numbers start hiding because you made them feel uncomfortable with all the staring?"

"Good point. Besides, if I'm even close, it's enough. All these kids being here is a much bigger deal."

Larisa had been correct in her righteous PA system takeover. This wasn't a system made for us. Girls and their needs were added as an afterthought. My voice alone couldn't save me no matter how loud and chaotic I went with it. But maybe the power of a tsunami of voices barreling over the board could get them to listen to our financial evidence.

There were kids and parents everywhere. Michael F. signed up new people to speak. Larisa helped some younger girls get their ideas onto note cards. Isabella worked the swag table. Someone cued up Joan Jett on the karaoke. Change felt possible.

"Ooh, the bubble machine is out," Gracie said. "Off to refill."

I watched her skip away, then heard a velvety voice behind me. "Hey."

I turned to see Ethan staring down at me.

"You here with the lacrosse bros to make fun of us?" I stood up to meet his eyes. Or as best I could, since I towered over him.

"Those guys won't show. At lunch is different," he said.

"What about you? Speaking at the meeting?" I asked.

"Just talking to you. Um, listen," he said. "I was a jerk. My sister was watching that video of Madison, and all the guys were over laughing. But after they left she told me about how important this all is, like, it would have made a difference when she was in middle school."

"You feel bad now because of a personal connection. I'm recovering from a similar ailment. The best medicine is to act," I said.

"I was going along, like, how much can it matter . . . I know I don't deserve a second chance."

Obviously. But it was more than that. He could just do something, anything. He had access to people in power that most of us could never dream of.

"Did you talk to your dad?" I asked.

"No, but my mom told him he should support what you're doing, and I was in the room when they were fighting, so can you and I just . . ."

That smile, those lashes, his bothering to come here and apologize.

He took a step closer. And another. My breath quickened. He leaned in toward my face. I knew then that it was happening. I seized the moment.

"Give me that jacket," I said.

He laughed. "Helen, I'm about to kiss you."

"I am fully aware of what is happening. And it is that you are giving me that jacket."

Ethan laughed again, but he stood up straight and took it off. He held it out, and I slid my arms in and tipped the collar up. It felt warm and wistful, like a fall day when the sun is so bright you mistake it for summer.

I turned to face Ethan, and he leaned in again. This time I put my hand up.

"You are not worthy of this jacket or me. Being a catch in the middle of this nonsense does not actually make you a catch. I'm saving this first kiss."

"Dude, Helen, what do I tell my mom? She bought me that jacket."

"Tell her it has gone in search of justice," I said. Then I turned and walked into the school.

Fifty people were waiting in the lobby outside the library for the meeting to start. The agenda taped to the locked door said 8:00 p.m. By 8:30, people were getting restless. That's when we found the county reporter.

"Hello, Intrepid Reporter Claudette Kang!" Gracie said.

"They're still in closed session?" Claudette asked.

"The meeting was supposed to start a half hour ago. We're still in 'casually late' territory. Maybe they're building the vibe," Gracie said.

Claudette shook her head. "The vibe is to wait you out. They're in closed session now. When they're supposed to cover things so sensitive that the public shouldn't hear it. Stuff like contract negotiations, firing someone. Only, you don't know what they're talking about, or how long it will take. They'll find reasons to stay in there until this crowd has given up and gone home."

"We won't leave," I said.

"I got you, but there's some kids on the younger side, parents who are probably paying a babysitter and can't stay forever. There's one of your rulers now, checking on whether his subjects have gone back to their hovels."

Claudette pointed to the double doors of the library, where Mr. Rogers had peeked his head out. His eyes got real big and he ducked back inside.

A half hour late turned into forty-five minutes late. People really were starting to leave. Even Claudette was packing up her bag.

"What do we do?" I asked her.

"Nothing you can do. This is how they operate. Too bad. You even got the local access news here."

This time I turned to find a camera operator and a woman with the most perfect hair and makeup ever pushing her way through the crowd. At the doors to the library, she turned to face the camera.

"Hang on," the camera guy said. "Who is in the shot?"

It was none other than the board president, peeking his head out.

"We're still in closed session," he said quickly.

But the local access reporter stuck her foot in the door. "I need to be up at 3:00 a.m. to cover traffic. Less than ten percent of the crowd has left. Time to get started, or I can always do a report on whether your board follows the open-meetings law."

The president closed the door with a humph.

"I love her," I hissed.

"Let's start a cult to her," Gracie agreed.

"Who are you weirdos worshipping now?" Madison asked, sliding in between us.

"Where have you been?" I said.

"I gave my first interview. To Ms. Durand in the vestibule. Great lighting there," Madison said.

Finally, the library doors opened again—all the way this time. The crowd streamed in and took seats in the rows of folding chairs facing the U-shaped dais. A plastic grin was plastered on every board member's face. They thought they could get through this. Something deep inside me knew they were wrong.

After calling the meeting to order, the board president said he wanted to clear some things up.

"You'll see on the agenda, an issue some people are discussing isn't on there. Of course, during public comment—"

"It's item B.3," said a voice in the back. I turned to see Gracie's Aunt Carmella sitting next to Claudette.

"There will be order!" said the president.

Carmella got up and went to the podium. It didn't matter that the mic wasn't on. The woman's voice carried to the ends of the earth. No wonder she could argue with dead people.

"You are voting on the contracts for paper and medical supplies," she said. "That includes the maxi pads, from what my niece tells me. Vote yes if your shriveled-up, money-wasting consciences tell you to, but do it in front of the children you're depriving and the free press who wants to know what you're up to."

The library erupted in cheers. Carmella motioned for everyone to be quiet.

"This isn't my fight. It belongs to the students. You should listen to them."

The news reporter stopped Carmella as she turned to go. "I'm Elisabeth Durand with RCKZ. Can I please interview you after the meeting?"

"My apologies to your waiting room viewers, but I promised an exclusive to the *Cambridge County Herald*," Carmella said. Then she bent down to Gracie and whispered, "Of course that exclusive will be my take on local chain pharmacies." Carmella laughed and then grabbed Gracie's cheeks in her hands. "You come over once school is out, we'll make the stromboli. Sometimes life can be easy and all the cheese stays on the inside."

Madison was at the podium. "Turn the mic on, please," she said with a smile that could sell dentures to a baby.

"We still have not started the agenda," yelled the president.

"I said 'on,' Derek," Madison spewed at the high school boy running audio-visual.

"You know the issue—we want period products in all the bathrooms. You know why it matters—because everyone who menstruates deserves period care. What you may not understand is that this change will also save money. We're here tonight to educate you on those issues. All of us."

"No, not all of us." One of the moms who'd complained about the bake sale flyers was standing and pushing her way up to the podium. I expected Madison to lose it, but she sneered at the woman and stepped aside.

"They want to put these pads in the boys' bathrooms," the mom said. "I am very careful about what I teach my sons. The state says I can opt them out of health class, and you can't let these kids usurp my power. This is a waste of taxpayer dollars and a violation of my parental rights. And there are a lot of parents here tonight who will say no to indoctrinating our children."

And then the most shocking thing happened. Madison did the opposite of butt-kissing. "Ma'am," she said, leaning in to share the mic, "you're answering no to a question that literally no one is asking."

"Young lady—" the superintendent began, but Madison was so over it.

"The question is, do you think any student should miss class because they're having a period and they don't have a maxi pad?" She turned to face the room. "Which of you will stand up and say yes to our faces? You think kids should miss class because of their period. Whether a few pads go into the boys' bathrooms is just one part about this much bigger issue, but it is a necessary part. Everyone who menstruates matters."

Then the second most unexpected thing happened. Madison pulled Michael F. up next to her.

He cleared his throat and addressed the board. "Right, now then. I'm a boys' bathroom user, which is something I never expected to say at a podium, and, um, I'm totally fine with the pads in the bathrooms. And most guys I talk to are like, whatever, we support it. But if any students are actually worried, that seems like something they have to talk through, rather than you using it as an excuse to keep pads from other kids. My classmates having periods don't get to say *I'm not comfortable with this* or *I don't want to think about menstruation*. There is this thing called the endometrium and it does not care what you have to say—"

Madison tapped Michael F. on the shoulder and gave him the universal sign for *wrap it up before things get weird*.

"In conclusion," he said, "no one is making anyone use the pads. They'll just be there. If the maxi pad aisle at the grocery store hasn't already indoctrinated your kid, I think they'll be okay." Somewhere, a turtle was pumping its little turtle fist.

Another mom went to get up, but Ms. Basset, the PTA president, gently pulled her back down into her seat by the shirttails. It felt like something in the air changed, like they realized they couldn't talk about us in the abstract, like pawns to hide behind on a chessboard, but as the real living beings who used these bathrooms, who this whole system was meant to serve. And that their names would be in the county paper, their faces on the flat screen in the dentist's office tomorrow morning for all their neighbors to see.

The superintendent called for order. We ignored him, stood

together, and lined up one after the other at the podium. Kids shared their emergency situations, the first time getting their period and having to run around begging for pads from other girls, the terror of not knowing what it was. Times they were told to see how the nurse could help when the budget at home meant compromises between food and toiletries. Gracie got to make her points on this being just the start of true period equity at school. The school nurse, Ms. Shapiro, even came and said she'd work with the business administrator and the custodians if they gave her a budget for pads.

Finally, after almost an hour, there was me. And me meant math. Mean math. But first I wanted to make a point.

"We shouldn't have to fundraise for necessities at school," I began. "If you think public education is a good thing, then you need to pay for what is required to attend school. By 'you' I of course mean 'us.' This isn't the school board's money. It doesn't even belong to the 'taxpayers.' These are public funds that are supposed to be spent on public good for everyone in this town. But I will do you one better here. The period products will fit in your existing budget."

Then I ran through the numbers for the board like I had for Madison. Except this time, I didn't convert it to normal human speak. I embraced their terms and documents and calculations to make it clear that if they tried to lie, I would catch them.

The only thing I left out was the fact that what we were asking for cost less than the new tackle sled they were set to approve that night for middle school football. That had been the most infuriating thing I'd found in all the budget documents. But for once, I thought maybe Ms. Varone was right about being strategic when you're the smartest person in the room. I was mad, but I was in control of how I used my mad.

There was a pause after I'd finished blasting them with numbers.

Then Ms. Laurent said, "Well. You certainly came back, didn't you." She almost sounded pleased. "This is impressive work, more financial and contract analysis than most adults do before asking us for a change. Next time do it without the mayhem first. Does this check out, Phil?"

The business administrator looked up from his computer. "Yes, I'm as shocked as you are." Then to me he said, "Did you find anywhere else we could achieve these kinds of savings?"

"Ahyeah," I said and sat down. If those chumps thought I was giving up the other fruits of my recreational math before they voted, they were out of touch with reality.

But of course, they were not. The practical need, the community desire, the fiscal basis, and most importantly, the county press were swirling around them. Even the dumbest fish knows you don't fight against a rip current. You give yourself to it and let the water push you out. There must have been some part of me hoping they would vote purely to help kids, rather than to save money and save face. I wanted to protect that little part of myself. It felt important.

The business administrator squinted at his screen again, then sat back and shrugged. "I say go for it. If it doesn't work out, we'll go back to the old way in next year's contract."

"I move that we vote," Ms. Laurent said.

The president banged his gavel. "There is nothing to vote on. None of this is on the agenda."

The crowd went wild, and not in a good way.

"Let's try this, then," Ms. Laurent said, raising her voice above everyone. "I move the board vote to remove the line item for individually boxed maxi pads from the contract listed at Agenda Item B.3 and that the business administrator work with the nurse to use those savings to procure the bulk, school-wide supply of, let's say, modern maxi pads for all middle school bathrooms. Is there a second?"

Two board members seconded. The business administrator called the roll. The vote passed 5–4. The no votes came from the school board president, a member concerned about amending the custodial job descriptions to accommodate pad distribution, another who refused to make any comment, and Mr. Rogers, who couldn't resist saying the quiet part out loud:

"I just don't think everyone should have to pay for this. As I've said, you girls will be paying for these products for decades. Start figuring it out now. All of you voting in favor of this will answer for it at the ballot box."

"I wonder when this guy's term is up," Gracie whispered to me.

"I wonder how old you have to be to run for school board," I said.

None of us sat through the rest of the meeting. Outside, the karaoke and bubble machines cranked up as kids hollered and high-fived. I couldn't stop smiling. It felt amazing. The energy of all those people getting it done.

Madison ran over and barreled me and Gracie into a group hug.

"We did it. It was a complete mess, and I totally violated every single one of Robert's Rules of Order, but it worked. The three pillars we came up with. I might turn that into a TED Talk on how to create change in your small town."

"Congratulations, Madison," Gracie said.

The way Madison looked at her, I thought maybe she could finally see the real Gracie. The swirling vortex of heart and creativity. The girl who saved all of us from ourselves and each other and found a way for us to work together and imagine a better future.

"This is going on the top of my résumé," Madison said, "and if you two ever wise up, you'll put it on the top of yours, too. I'm running home to rethink my list of top college possibilities."

After Madison left, Mom came over and put her hand on my shoulder. She hadn't told me she was coming, and I was twice as shocked when she said, "That was amazing, Helen. You used math for good for a change."

She was getting teary. That was too much.

"Come on, Mom. I promise to do something bad with math soon. Gracie and I are designing a slide from her second-floor bedroom into a kiddie pool this summer."

"Filled with nacho cheese, of course," Gracie said.

"When the school said you had to accomplish something, and then there was all that chaos as usual . . . I don't know. Soon young people will have always seen pads out in the open, before they ever even get their first period. It will normalize it."

I gasped. "Mom, are you going to put your tampons on the counter at home?"

"Don't be fresh now after you did so good."

"I plan on making a sash of tampons like a beauty queen over summer break. Speaking of break and unspeakable sorrow and the end of the universe, does this mean Helen doesn't have to go to Sage Academy?" Gracie said.

I understood why she asked. But I didn't want to deal with it. I was actually glad when Mom punted.

"No, it does not mean that. I'll be in the car, and I'll text your moms I'm driving you home, Gracie. But no rush. Enjoy this. And make sure you clean the whole place up."

If there's one thing worse than having to clean you room, it's cleaning outside. Pink tinsel may be pretty, but it gets everywhere, and Isabella spent half the night lecturing me on what it would do to a turtle if those strands ever made their way to the ocean. But we got it all done as a group, even as the school board members streamed out of the building, some giving us a thumbs-up, others avoiding eye contact. And then it was just me and Gracie packing up the swag table. That is, until Ms. Varone joined us.

Gracie squealed. "You came after all!"

"I needed final approval for the HVAC compressors," she said and pointed to a massive binder tucked under her arm.

"And?" Gracie said.

Ms. Varone laughed. "Approved. Thank you for asking. And you girls did it. You still ended up punished, and now I have to create a commission on free speech in schools to figure out how to deal with the debates you caused."

"What if you had it to do all over again?" I asked.

"If I had it to do all over again, I'd go to law school. If I had this particular thing to do over again, I would have separated the two of you instead of assigning the caring project. Girls, you won, which is great, but not in the right way."

I knew she was correct, but not right. Mostly, I didn't care. There would be plenty of time to learn to do things the correct way, or better yet, change what people considered correct. For now, I was happy to have finally done some good.

"It is getting late, so let me leave you with this parting advice for high school," Ms. Varone said. A few seconds passed. She smiled at us. And then she walked away.

And that is when it hit me.

"Is that what I think it is?" Gracie whispered.

"It's making me tear up," I said.

A fart so virulent, with such staying power, with such tenacity that it didn't even move in that warm spring air. A whole field of lavender couldn't have covered it up.

"Gracie, come on, let's get your stuff in the car and get out of here."

"No, Helen, let's swim in it. I want to remember this. This is the smell of accomplishing something in middle school."

AUTHOR'S NOTE

Thank you so much for reading Helen and Gracie's story! They are the chaos monsters of my heart. One reason I love them: they're completely themselves always, which means they make messy mistakes on their way to creating change (plus I also have a long-standing personal relationship with soft cheeses #brie-4life). That is how progress happens in real life, too.

When it comes to health equity issues, writing books, making videos about crochet uteruses and flying tampons, turning graham crackers into Maxi-Grahams for my family, and sharing my personal experiences with friends are all just as important to me as meeting with my government representatives. Breaking down stigma to make it more comfortable to talk about tough topics is right up there with taking official actions. And chatting is right up there with eating chips on my list of favorite things to do.

Advocacy doesn't have to be fancy or formal. You don't need special training or perfect research. If you're interested in period justice, you can start by thinking about your own experiences and learning what resources are actually available at your school. Then consider what you already love to do: write a story, make art, create 10-point plans like Madison, construct an argument like Larisa, rally everyone like Isabella, or get together with your friends to complain until you finally decide to do something about it. Oh, I love that last one so much. My point is that you truly can make a difference by using what is special about you.

Helen and Gracie may be fictional, but real students around the country have been advocating for menstrual equity for years after experiencing a personal need or recognizing a need in their community. When I started writing this book nearly a decade ago while trying to figure out how to talk about periods in a positive way as a parent, I was thrilled to learn that a few districts had pilot programs for pads in schools, and student groups and troops were collecting pads to share with each other. This was something I couldn't have even imagined growing up. Now, the movement is stronger than ever with numerous states requiring some pads in schools and/or providing some funding for them. All thanks to students like you and their allies.

This progress gives me hope that we'll all move toward period justice in the future, but right now whether you have what you need depends on where you live. Even in places where pads are required, they aren't always stocked. And some schools that aren't required to by law still make pads available. There is a patchwork of district, local, county, and state laws and funding to navigate, but there is also lots of good news! You and your friends are in the best position to know what is happening in your school. You can connect with student groups and nonprofit organizations already working on period equity in your state for resources, and you can ask your state representative's office to explain what is required by your state and what new laws are in the works to improve things. You are not alone, and you don't have to start from scratch.

If you're interested in more resources, please feel free to visit aliterese.com, where you can find activity sheets on taking action, recipes for the Endo-TREAT-rium's delightfully disgusting desserts, and how-to handouts for crafts from the world of FREE PERIOD!

ACKNOWLEDGMENTS

Thank you to the inspiring students and their allies fighting for menstrual and period equity and justice in their schools and beyond. I am in awe of all you have and will accomplish!

Thank you to my hilarious and supportive family for reading every page, cheering every small victory, and supporting me through every hiccup along the way. This book would not exist without all you've done for me over the near decade it has taken to get from first draft to publication. I love you so much.

Thank you to my agent, editor, and the entire team at Scholastic and their partners who made this book possible.

Thank you to my mentor, critique group, beta readers, check-in partners, fellow writers, family, and friends who read pages and chatted with me about books, menstruation, and the power of fart jokes.

And thank you for taking the time to read this book! I hope you had fun!